I stepped cautiously ⟨...⟩ ⟨...⟩
big that it was hard t⟨...⟩ ⟨...⟩
girl who lay under it, ⟨...⟩ ⟨...⟩ ⟨...⟩ing
hunch. I gingerly r⟨...⟩ ⟨...⟩y finger-tips and
pressed it. It seemed ⟨...⟩ and distended, but there was a
sensation of something slithery inside. In fact, it felt exactly
like the stomach of a pregnant woman.

'Can't you just kill it?' I asked Dr Hughes. 'It must be the
size of a small child by now. Can't you just stick a scalpel
into it?'

Dr Hughes shook his head. 'I wish I could. I'd like to
chop it off with a meat cleaver, if you want to know the
truth. But every X-ray shows that the nervous system of this
creature is inextricably bound up to Karen's nervous system. Any attempt to remove it would kill her at once.
They're not so much like mother and child – they're more
like Siamese twins . . .'

Dr Hughes tucked his hands in the pockets of his robe and
looked sadly down at his dying patient. 'She hasn't lost any
weight at all – but she hasn't gained any either. Whatever
this tumour is, it's taking all its sustenance directly from her.
Every ounce it grows, it takes from Karen.'

Graham Masterton

# THE MANITOU

**A STAR BOOK**
*published by*
*the Paperback Division of*
W. H. ALLEN & Co. Ltd

A Star Book
Published in 1977
by the Paperback Division of W. H. Allen & Co. Ltd
A Howard and Wyndham Company
123 King Street, London W6 9JG

First published in Great Britain by
Neville Spearman Ltd, 1975

Copyright © 1975 Graham Masterton

Printed in Great Britain by
Cox and Wyman Ltd, London, Reading and Fakenham

ISBN 0 352 39616 4

# CONTENTS

'On being ask'd what ye Daemon look'd like,
the antient Wonder-Worker Misquamacus covered
his face so that onlie ye Eyes look'd out,
and then gave a very curious and Circumstantiall
Relation, saying it was sometimes small and
solid, like a Great Toad ye Bigness of many
Ground-Hogs, but sometimes big and cloudy,
with no Shape, though with a face which had
Serpents grown from it.'

H. P. LOVECRAFT

# PRELUDE

The phone bleeped. Without looking up, Dr Hughes sent his hand across his desk in search of it. The hand scrabbled through sheafs of paper, bottles of ink, week-old newspapers and crumpled sandwich packets. It found the telephone, and picked it up.

Dr Hughes put it to his ear. He looked peaky-faced and irritated, like a squirrel trying to store away its nuts.

'*Hughes! This is McEvoy.*'

'Well? I'm sorry, Dr McEvoy, I'm very busy.'

'*I didn't mean to interrupt you in your work, Dr Hughes. But I have a patient down here whose condition should interest you.*'

Dr Hughes sniffed and took off his rimless glasses.

'What kind of condition?' he asked. 'Listen, Dr McEvoy, it's very considerate of you to call me, but I have paperwork as high as a mountain up here, and I really can't—'

McEvoy wasn't put off. '*Well, I really think you'll be interested, Dr Hughes. You're interested in tumours, aren't you? Well, we've got a tumour down here to end all tumours.*'

'What's so terrific about it?'

'*It's sited on the back of the neck. The patient is a female Caucasian, twenty-three years old. No previous record of tumorous growth, either benign or malignant.*'

'And?'

'*It's moving,*' said Dr McEvoy. '*The tumour is actually moving, like there's something under the skin that's alive.*'

Dr Hughes was doodling flowers with his ballpen. He frowned for a moment, then said: 'X-ray?'

'*Results in twenty minutes.*'

'Palpitation?'

'*Feels like any other tumour. Except that it squirms.*'

'Have you tried lancing it? Could be just an infection.'

'*I'll wait and see the X-ray first of all.*'

Dr Hughes sucked thoughtfully at the end of his pen. His mind flicking back over all the pages of all the medical books he had ever absorbed, seeking a parallel case, or a precedent, or even something remotely connected to the idea of a *moving* tumour. Maybe he was tired, but somehow he couldn't seem to slot the idea in anywhere.

'*Dr Hughes?*'

'Yeah, I'm still here. Listen, what time do you have?'

'*Ten after three.*'

'Okay, Dr McEvoy. I'll come down.'

He laid down the telephone and sat back in his chair and rubbed his eyes. It was St Valentine's Day, and outside in the streets of New York City the temperature had dropped to eight degrees centigrade and there was six inches of snow on the ground. The sky was metallic and overcast, and the traffic crept about on muffled wheels. From the eighteenth storey of the Sisters of Jerusalem Hospital, the city had a weird and luminous quality that he'd never seen before. It was like being on the moon, thought Dr Hughes. Or the end of the world. Or the Ice Age.

There was trouble with the heating system, and he had left his overcoat on. He sat there under the puddle of light from his desklamp, an exhausted young man of thirty-three, with a nose as sharp and pointy as a scalpel, and a scruffy shock of dark brown hair. He looked more like a teenage auto mechanic than a national expert on malignant tumours.

His office door swung open and a plump, white-haired lady with upswept red spectacles came in, bearing a sheaf of paper and a cup of coffee.

'Just a little more paperwork, Dr Hughes. And I thought you'd like something to warm you up.'

'Thank you, Mary.' He opened the new file that she had brought him, and sniffed more persistently. 'Jesus, have you seen this stuff? I'm supposed to be a consultant, not a filing clerk. Listen, take this back and dump it on Dr Ridgeway. He *likes* paper. He likes it better than flesh and blood.'

Mary shrugged. 'Dr Ridgeway *sent* it to *you*.'

Dr Hughes stood up. In his overcoat, he looked like Charlie Chaplin in *The Gold Rush*. He waved the file around in exasperation, and it knocked over his single Valentine's card, which he knew had been sent by his mother.

'Oh ... Okay. I'll have a look at it later. I'm going down to see Dr McEvoy. He has a patient he wants me to look at.'

'Will you be long, Dr Hughes?' asked Mary. 'You have a meeting at four-thirty.'

Dr Hughes stared at her wearily, as though he was wondering who she was.

'Long? No, I don't think so. Just as long as it takes.'

He stepped out of his office into the neon-lit corridor. The Sisters of Jerusalem was an expensive private hospital, and never smelled of anything as functional as carbolic and chloroform. The corridors were carpeted in thick red plush, and there were fresh-cut flowers at every corner. It was more like the kind of hotel where middle-aged executives take their secretaries for a week-end of strenuous sin.

Dr Hughes called an elevator and sank to the fifteenth floor. He stared at himself in the elevator mirror, and he considered he was looking more sick than some of his patients. Perhaps he would take a vacation. His mother had always liked Florida, or maybe they could visit his sister in San Diego.

He went through two sets of swing doors, and into Dr McEvoy's office. Dr McEvoy was a short, heavily-built man whose white coats were always far too tight under his arms. He looked like a surgical sausage. His face was big and moon-like and speckled, with a snub little Irish nose. He had once played football for the hospital team, until he had fractured his kneecap in a violent tackle. Nowadays, he walked with a slightly over-dramatized limp.

'Glad you came down,' he smiled. 'This really is very peculiar, and I know you're the world's greatest expert.'

'Hardly,' said Dr Hughes. 'But thanks for the compliment.'

Dr McEvoy stuck his finger in his ear and screwed it around with great thoughtfulness and care. 'The X-rays will be here in five or ten minutes. Meanwhile, I can't think what else I can do.'

'Can you show me the patient?' asked Dr Hughes.

'Of course. She's in my ante-room. I should take your overcoat off if I were you. She might think I brought you in off the street.'

Dr Hughes hung up his shapeless black coat, and then followed Dr McEvoy through to the brightly-lit ante-room. There were armchairs and magazines and flowers, and a fish-tank full of bright tropical fish. Through the venetian blinds, Dr Hughes could see the odd metallic radiance of the after-noon snow.

In a corner of the room, reading a copy of *Sunset*, was a slim dark-haired girl. She had a squarish, delicate face – a bit like an imp, thought Dr Hughes. She was wearing a plain coffee-coloured dress that made her cheeks look rather sallow. The only clue to her nervousness was an ashtray crammed with cigarette butts, and a haze of smoke in the air.

'Miss Tandy,' said Dr McEvoy, 'this is Dr Hughes. Dr Hughes is an expert on conditions of your kind, and he would just like to take a look at you and ask you a few questions.'

Miss Tandy laid aside her magazine and smiled. 'Sure,' she said, in a distinctive New England accent. Good family, thought Dr Hughes. He didn't have to guess if she was wealthy or not. You just didn't seek treatment at the Sister of Jerusalem Hospital unless you had more cash than you could raise off the floor.

'Lean forward,' said Dr Hughes. Miss Tandy bent over, and Dr Hughes lifted the hair at the back of her neck.

Right in the hollow of her neck was a smooth round bulge, about the size and shape of a glass paperweight. Dr Hughes ran his fingers over it, and it seemed to have the normal texture of a benign fibrous growth.

'How long have you had this?' he asked.

'Two or three days,' said Miss Tandy. 'I made an ap-pointment as soon as it started to grow. I was frightened it was – well, cancer or something.'

Dr Hughes looked across at Dr McEvoy and frowned.

'Two or three *days*? Are you sure?'

'Exactly,' said Miss Tandy. 'Today is Friday, isn't it? Well, I first felt it when I woke up on Tuesday morning.'

Dr Hughes squeezed the tumour gently in his hand. It was firm, and hard, but he couldn't detect any movement.

'Does that hurt?' he asked.

'There's a kind of a prickling sensation. But that's about all.'

Dr McEvoy said: 'She felt the same thing when I squeezed it.'

Dr Hughes let Miss Tandy's hair fall back, and told her she could sit up straight again. He pulled up an armchair, and found a tatty scrap of paper in his pocket, and started to jot down a few notes as he talked to her.

'How big was the tumour when you first noticed it?'

'Very small. About the size of a butter-bean, I guess.'

'Did it grow all the time, or only at special times?'

'It only seems to grow at night. I mean, every morning I wake up and it's bigger.'

Dr Hughes made a detailed squiggle on his piece of paper.

'Can you feel it normally. I mean, can you feel it now?'

'It doesn't seem to be any worse than any other kind of bump. But sometimes I get the feeling that it's *shifting*.'

The girl's eyes were dark, and there was more fear in them than her voice was giving away.

'Well,' she said slowly. 'It's almost like somebody trying to get comfortable in bed. You know – sort of shifting around, and then lying still.'

'How often does this happen?'

She looked worried. She could sense the bafflement in Dr Hughes, and that worried her.

'I don't know. Maybe four or five times a day.'

Dr Hughes made some more notes and chewed his lip.

'Miss Tandy, have you noticed any changes in your own personal condition of health over the past few days – since you've had this tumour?'

'Only a little tiredness. I guess I don't sleep too well at night. But I haven't lost any weight or anything like that.'

'Hmm.' Dr Hughes wrote some more, and looked for a

while at what he'd written. 'How much do you smoke?'

'Usually only half a pack a day. I'm not a great smoker. I'm just nervous right now, I guess.'

Dr McEvoy said: 'She had a chest X-ray not long ago. She had a clean bill of health.'

Dr Hughes said: 'Miss Tandy, do you live alone? Where do you live?'

'I'm staying with my aunt on 82nd Street. I'm working for a record company, as a personal assistant. I wanted to find an apartment of my own, but my parents thought it would be a good idea if I lived with my aunt for a while. She's sixty-two. She's a wonderful old lady. We get along together just fine.'

Dr Hughes lowered his head. 'Don't get me wrong when I ask this, Miss Tandy, but I think you'll understand why I have to. Is your aunt in a good state of health, and is the apartment clean? There's no health-risk there, like cockroaches or blocked drains or food dirt?'

Miss Tandy almost grinned, for the first time since Dr Hughes had seen her. 'My aunt is a wealthy woman, Dr Hughes. She has a full-time cleaner, and a maid to help with the cooking and entertaining.'

Dr Hughes nodded. 'Okay, we'll leave it like that for now. Let's go and chase up those X-rays, Dr McEvoy.'

They went back into Dr McEvoy's office and sat down. Dr McEvoy took out a stick of chewing-gum and bent it between his teeth.

'What do you make of it, Dr Hughes?'

Dr Hughes sighed. 'At the moment, I don't make anything at all. This bump came up in two or three days, and I've never come across a tumour that did that before. Then there's this sensation of movement. Have you felt it move yourself?'

'Sure,' said Dr McEvoy. 'Just a slight shifting, like there was something under there.'

'That may be caused by movements of the neck. But we can't really tell until we see the X-rays.'

They sat in silence for a few minutes, with the noises of the hospital leaking faintly from the building all around them. Dr Hughes felt cold and weary, and wondered when he was going to get home. He had been up until 2 a.m. last night, dealing with files and statistics, and it looked as though he was going to be just as late tonight. He sniffed, and stared at his scuffy brown shoe on the carpet.

After five or six minutes, the office door opened and the radiologist came in with a large brown envelope. She was a tall negress with short-cut hair and no sense of humour at all.

'What do you make of them, Selena?' asked Dr McEvoy, taking the envelope across the room to his light-box.

'I'm not sure at all, Dr McEvoy. It's clear enough, but it doesn't make any kind of sense.'

Dr McEvoy took out the black X-ray film and clipped it up. He switched on the light, and they had a view of the back of Miss Tandy's skull, from the side. There was the tumour all right – a large shadowy lump. But inside it, instead of the normal fibrous growth, there seemed to be a small tangled knot of tissue and bone.

'See here,' said Dr McEvoy, pointing with his ballpen. 'There seem to be roots of some kind, bony roots, holding the inside of the tumour against the neck. Now what the hell do you think that is?'

'I haven't the slightest idea,' said Dr Hughes. 'I've never seen anything remotely like this before. It doesn't seem like a tumour at all.'

Dr McEvoy shrugged. 'Okay, it's not a tumour. So what is it?'

Dr Hughes peered closely at the X-ray. The little knot of tissue and bone was too formless and mixed-up to make any sense out of it. There was only one thing to do, and that was to operate. Cut it out, and examine it in the open. And at the rate it was growing, that operation had better be done quickly.

Dr Hughes picked up the telephone on Dr McEvoy's desk. 'Mary? Listen I'm still down here with Dr McEvoy. Would you see how soon Dr Snaith has a space available for surgery? I have something here that needs urgent attention. That's right. Yes, a tumour. But it's very malignant, and there might be problems if we don't operate fast. That's it. Thanks.'

'Malignant?' said Dr McEvoy. 'How do we know it's malignant?'

Dr Hughes shook his head. 'We *don't* know, but until we find out whether it's dangerous or harmless, I'm going to treat it as dangerous.'

'I just wish I knew what the hell it was,' said Dr McEvoy gloomily. 'I've been right through the medical dictionary, and there just isn't anything like it.'

Dr Hughes grinned tiredly. 'Maybe it's a new disease. Maybe they'll name it after you. McEvoy's Malady. Fame at last. You always wanted to be famous, didn't you?'

'Right now I'd settle for a cup of coffee and a hot beef sandwich. The Nobel Prize I can have any time.'

The phone bleeped. Dr Hughes picked it up.

'Mary? Oh, right. Okay, that's fine. Yes, that'll do fine. Tell Dr Snaith thank you.'

'He's free?' asked Dr McEvoy.

'Tomorrow morning, 10 a.m. I better go and tell Miss Tandy.'

Dr Hughes pushed through the double doors into the ante-room, and Miss Tandy was still sitting there, half-way through another cigarette, and staring, without seeing, at the open magazine on her lap.

'Miss Tandy?'

She looked up quickly. 'Oh, yes,' she said.

Dr Hughes drew up a chair and sat down next to her with his hands clasped in front of him. He tried to look serious and steady and reliable, to calm her obvious fright, but he was so tired that he didn't succeed in looking anything but morbid.

'Listen, Miss Tandy, I think we'll have to operate. It doesn't look as though this swelling is anything to worry about, but at the rate it's been growing, I'd like to see it removed as soon as possible, and I guess you would too.'

She raised her hand towards the back of her neck, then dropped it and nodded. 'I understand. Of course.'

'If you can be here by eight o'clock tomorrow morning,

I'll have Dr Snaith remove it for you around ten. Dr Snaith is a very fine surgeon, and he has years of experience with tumours like yours.'

Miss Tandy attempted to smile. 'That's very kind of you. Thank you.'

Dr Hughes shrugged. 'Don't thank me. I'm only doing my job. But, listen, I don't think you have anything to worry about. I won't pretend that your condition is not unusual, because it is. But part of our profession is dealing with unusual conditions. You've come to the right place.'

Miss Tandy stubbed out her cigarette and gathered her things together.

'Will I need anything special?' she asked. 'A couple of nightdresses, I suppose, and a wrap?'

Dr Hughes nodded. 'Bring some slippers, too. You're not going to be exactly bedridden.'

'Okay,' she said, and Dr Hughes showed her out. He watched her walk quickly down the corridor to the elevator, and he thought how slim and young and elf-like she looked. He wasn't one of those specialists who thought of his patients in terms of their condition and nothing else – not like Dr Pawson, the lung specialist, who could remember individual ailments long after he'd forgotten the faces that went with them. Life is more than an endless parade of lumps and bumps, thought Dr Hughes. At least I hope it is.

He was still standing in the corridor when Dr McEvoy poked his moon-like face round the door.

'Dr Hughes?'

'Yes?'

'Come inside a moment, take a look at this.'

He followed Dr McEvoy tiredly into his office. While he had been talking to Miss Tandy, Dr McEvoy had been looking through his medical reference books, and there were diagrams and X-rays strewn around all over his desk.

'You found something?' asked Dr Hughes.

'I don't know. It seems to be as ridiculous as anything else in this case.'

Dr McEvoy handed him a heavy textbook, opened at a page covered with charts and diagrams. Dr Hughes frowned, and examined them carefully, and then he went over to the light-box and peered at the pictures of Miss Tandy's skull again.

'That's crazy,' he said.

Dr McEvoy stood there with his hands on his hips and nodded. 'You're quite right. It is crazy. But you have to admit, it looks pretty much like it.'

Dr Hughes shut the book. 'But even if you're right – in *two days*?'

'Well, if *this* is possible, *anything* is possible.'

'If *this* is possible, the Red Sox will win the next series.'

The two pale doctors stood in their office on the fifteenth floor of the hospital and looked at the X-rays and just didn't know what to say next.

'Perhaps it's a hoax?' said Dr McEvoy.

Dr Hughes shook his head. 'No way. How could it be? And what for?'

'I don't know. People dream up hoaxes for all kinds of reasons.'

'Can you think of a reason for this?'

Dr McEvoy grimaced. 'Can you believe it's real?'

'I don't know,' replied Dr Hughes. 'Maybe it is. Maybe it's the one case in a million that's really real.'

They opened the book again, and studied the X-ray again, and the more they compared the diagrams with Miss Tandy's tumour, the more resemblance they discovered.

According to *Clinical Gynaecology*, the knot of tissue and bone that Miss Tandy was harbouring in the back of her neck was a human foetus, of a size that suggested it was about eight weeks old.

# CHAPTER ONE

# OUT OF THE NIGHT

If you think it's an easy life being a mystic, you ought to try telling fifteen fortunes a day, at $25 a time, and then see whether you're quite so keen on it.

At the same moment that Karen Tandy was consulting Dr Hughes and Dr McEvoy at the Sisters of Jerusalem Hospital, I was giving old Mrs Winconis a quick tour of her immediate prospects with the help of the Tarot cards.

We were sitting round the green baize table in my Tenth Avenue flat, with the drapes drawn tight and the incense smouldering suggestively in the corner, and my genuine simulated antique oil-lamp casting pretty mysterious shadows. Mrs Winconis was wrinkled and old and smelled of musty perfume and fox-fur coats, and she came around every Friday evening for a detailed rundown of the seven days ahead.

As I laid out the cards in the Celtic cross, she fidgeted and sniffed and peered across at me like a moth-eaten ermine scenting its prey. I knew she was dying to ask me what I saw, but I never gave any hints until the whole thing was set out on the table. The more suspense, the better. I had to go through the whole performance of frowning and sighing, and biting my lips, and making out that I was in communication with the powers from beyond. After all, that's what she paid her $25 for.

But she couldn't resist the temptation. As the last card went down, she leaned forward and asked: 'What is it, Mr Erskine? What do you see? Is there anything about Daddy?'

'Daddy' was her name for Mr Winconis, a fat and dour old supermarket manager who chain-smoked cigars and didn't believe in anything more mystical than the first three runners at Aqueduct. Mrs Winconis never suggested as much, but it was plain from the way she talked that her greatest hope in life was for Daddy's heart to give out, and the Winconis fortune to come her way.

I looked at the cards with my usual elaborate concentration. I knew as much about the Tarot as anybody did who had taken the trouble to read *Tarot Made Easy*, but it was the style that carried it off. If you want to be a mystic, which is actually easier than being an advertising copywriter, or a summer camp warden, or a coach-tour guide, then you have to *look* like a mystic.

Since I am a rather mousy thirty-two-year-old from Cleveland, Ohio, with the beginnings of a bald patch underneath my scrubby brown hair, and a fine but overlarge nose in my fine but pallid face, I took the trouble to paint my eyebrows into satanic arches, and wear an emerald satin cloak with moons and stars sewn on it, and perch a triangular green hat on my head. The hat used to have a badge on it that said *GREEN BAY PACKERS*, but I took it off, for obvious reasons.

I invested in incense, and a few leather-bound copies of the *Encyclopaedia Britannica*, and a beaten-up old skull from a second-hand store in the Village, and then I placed an advertisement in the newspapers which read: 'The Incredible Erskine – Fortunes Read, Future Foretold, Your Fate Revealed.'

Within a couple of months, I was handling more business than I knew what to do with, and for the first time in my life I was able to afford a new Mercury Cougar and a quad stereo with earphones to match. But, as I say, it wasn't easy. The constant tide of middle-aged ladies who came simpering into my apartment, dying to hear what was going to happen in their tedious middle-aged lives, was almost enough to drown me forever in the well of human despair.

'Well?' said Mrs Winconis, clutching her alligator pocketbook in her wrinkled old fingers. 'What can you *see*, Mr Erskine?'

I shook my head slowly and magnificently. 'The cards are solemn today, Mrs Winconis. They carry many warnings. They tell you that you are pressing too hard towards a future that, when it comes to pass, you may not enjoy as much as you thought. I see a portly gentleman with a cigar – it must be Daddy. He is saying something in great sorrow. He is saying something about money.'

'What is he saying? Do the cards tell you what he is saying?' whispered Mrs Winconis. Whenever I mentioned 'money', she started to twitch and jump like spit on a red-hot stove. I've seen some pretty ugly lusts in my time, but the lust for money in middle-aged women is enough to make you lose your lunch.

'He is saying that something is too expensive,' I went on, in my special hollow voice. 'Something is definitely too expensive. I know what it is. I can see what it is. He is saying that canned salmon is too expensive He doesn't think that people will want to buy it at that price.'

'Oh,' said Mrs Winconis, vexed. But I knew what I was doing. I had checked the price-rise column in the *Supermarket Report* that morning, and I knew that canned salmon was due for an increase. Next week, when Daddy started complaining about it, Mrs Winconis would remember my words, and be mightily impressed with my incredible clairvoyant talents.

'What about *me*?' asked Mrs Winconis. 'What is going to happen to *me*?'

I stared gloomily at the cards.

'Not a good week, I'm afraid. Not a good week at all. On Monday you will have an accident. Not a serious one. Nothing worse than dropping a heavy weight on your foot, but it will be painful. It will keep you awake Monday night. On Tuesday, you will play bridge with your friends as usual. Someone will cheat you, but you will not discover who it is. So keep your stakes small, and don't take any risks. Wednesday you will have an unpleasant telephone call, possibly obscene. Thursday you will eat a meal that does not agree with you, and you will wish that you never ate it.'

Mrs Winconis fixed me with her dull grey eyes. 'Is it really that bad?' she asked.

'It doesn't have to be. Remember that the cards can warn

as well as foretell. If you take steps to avoid these pitfalls, you will not necessarily have such a bad week.'

'Well, thank God for that,' she said. 'It's worth the money just to know what to look out for.'

'The spirits think well of you, Mrs Winconis,' I said, in my special voice. 'They care for you, and would not like to see you discomfited or harmed. If you treat the spirits right, they will treat you right.'

She stood up. 'Mr Erskine, I don't know how to thank you. I'd best be getting along now, but I'll see you next week, won't I?'

I smiled my secret smile. 'Of course, Mrs Winconis. And don't forget your mystic motto for the week.'

'Oh, no, of course not. What is it this week, Mr Erskine?'

I opened a tattered old book that I kept on the table next to me. 'Your mystic motto for this week is: "Guard well the pips, and the fruit shall grow without let".'

She stood there for a moment with a far-away smile on her withered old face. 'That's beautiful, Mr Erskine. I shall repeat it every morning when I wake up. Thank you for a wonderful, wonderful session.'

'The pleasure,' I said, 'is all mine.'

I showed her to the elevator, taking care that none of my neighbours saw me in my ridiculous green cloak and hat, and waved her a fond farewell. As soon as she had sunk out of sight, I went back into my flat, switched on the light, blew out the incense, and turned on the television. With any luck, I wouldn't have missed too much of *Kojak*.

I was just going to the icebox to fetch myself a can of beer when the telephone rang. I tucked the receiver under my chin, and opened up the beer as I talked. The voice on the other end was female (of course) and nervous (of course). Only nervous females sought the services of a man like the Incredible Erskine.

'Mr Erskine?'

'Erskine's the name, fortune-telling's the game.'

'Mr Erskine, I wonder if I could come round and see you.'

'Of course, of course. The fee is twenty-five dollars for your ordinary glimpse into the immediate future, thirty

20

dollars for a year's forecast, fifty dollars for a lifetime review.'

'I just want to know what's going to happen *tomorrow*.' the voice sounded young, and very worried. I took a quick mental guess at a pregnant and abandoned secretary.

'Well, madam, that's my line. What time do you want to come?'

'Around nine? Is that too late?'

'Nine is fine, and the pleasure's mine. Can I have your name please?'

'Tandy. Karen Tandy. Thank you, Mr Erskine. I'll see you at nine.'

It might seem strange to you that an intelligent girl like Karen Tandy should seek help from a terrible quack like me, but until you've been dabbling in clairvoyance for quite a while, you don't realize how vulnerable people feel when they're threatened by things they don't understand. This is particularly true of illness and death, and most of my clients have some kind of question about their own mortality to ask. No matter how reassuring and competent a surgeon may be, he can't give people any answers when it comes to what is going to happen if their lives are suddenly snuffed out.

It's no good a doctor saying: 'Well, see here, madam, if your brain ceases to give out any more electronic impulses, we'll have to consider that you are lost and gone forever.'

Death is too frightening, too *total*, too mystical, for people to *want* to believe it has anything to do with the facts of medicine and surgery. They want to believe in a life after death, or at the very least in a spirit world, where the mournful ghosts of their long-dead ancestors roam about in the celestial equivalent to silk pyjamas.

I could see the fear of death on Karen Tandy's face when she knocked at my door. In fact, it was so strongly marked that I felt less than comfortable in my green cloak and my funny little green hat. She was delicately-boned and pointy-faced, the sort of girl who always won races in high school athletics, and she spoke with a grave politeness that made me feel more fraudulent than ever.

'Are you Mr Erskine?' she asked.

'That's me. Fortunes read, futures foretold. You know the rest.'

She walked quietly into my room and looked around at the incense burner and the yellowed skull and the close-drawn drapes. I suddenly felt that the whole set-up was incredibly phoney and false, but she didn't seem to notice. I drew out a chair for her to sit on, and offered her a cigarette. When I lit it, I could see that her hands were trembling.

'All right, Miss Tandy,' I asked her. 'What's the problem?'

'I don't know how to explain it, really. I've been to the hospital already, and they're going to give me an operation tomorrow morning. But there are all kinds of things I couldn't tell them about.'

I sat back and smiled encouragingly. 'Why don't you try telling me?'

'It's very difficult,' she said, in her soft, light voice. 'I get the feeling that it's something – much more than it seems.'

'Well,' I said, crossing my legs under my green silk robe. 'Would you like to tell me what it is?'

She raised her hand shyly to the back of her neck. 'About three days ago – Tuesday morning I think it was – I began to feel a kind of irritation there, at the back of my neck. It swelled up, and I was worried in case it was something serious, and I went to the hospital to have it looked at.'

'I see,' I said sympathetically. Sympathy, as you can probably guess, accounts for ninety-eight per cent of anyone's success as a clairvoyant. 'And what did the doctors tell you?'

'They said it was nothing to worry about, but at the same time they seemed pretty anxious to take it off.'

I smiled. 'So where do I come in?'

'Well, my aunt's been to see you once or twice. Mrs Karmann, I live with her. She doesn't know I'm here, but she's always said how good you are, and so I thought I could try you myself.'

Well, it was nice to know that my occult services were being praised abroad. Mrs Karmann was a lovely old lady who believed that her dead husband was always trying to get in touch with her from the spirit world. She came to see me

22

two or three times a month, whenever the dear departed Mr Karmann sent her a message from beyond. It happened in her dreams, she always told me. She heard him whispering in a strange language in the middle of the night, and that was the signal for her to trot over to Tenth Avenue and spend a few dollars with me. Very good business, Mrs Karmann.

'You want me to read your cards?' I asked, raising one of my devilishly arched eyebrows.

Karen Tandy shook her head. She looked more serious and worried than almost any client I could remember. I hoped she wasn't going to ask me to do something that required real occult talent.

'It's the dreams, Mr Erskine. Ever since this bump has started growing, I've had terrible dreams. The first night, I thought it was just an ordinary nightmare, but I've had the same dream every night, and each night it's been clearer. I don't even know if I want to go to bed tonight, because I just know I'm going to have the same dream, and it's going to be even more vivid, and very much worse.'

I pulled thoughtfully at the end of my nose. It was a habit of mine whenever I was pondering over something, and probably accounted for the size of my schonk. Some people scratch their heads when they think, and get dandruff. I just tug at my hooter.

'Miss Tandy, a lot of people have recurring dreams. It usually means that they're worrying about the same thing over and over. I don't think it's anything to get het up about.'

She stared at me with those big, deep, chocolate-brown eyes. 'It's not that kind of dream, Mr Erskine, I'm sure. It's too *real*. With the ordinary sort of dream, you feel it's all happening inside your head. But with this one, it seems to happen all around me, *outside me*, as well as inside my brain.'

'Well,' I said, 'supposing you tell me what it is.'

'It always starts the same way. I dream I'm standing on a strange island. It's winter, and there's a very cold wind blowing. I can feel that wind, even though the windows are always closed in my bedroom. It's night-time, and the moon

23

is up there behind the clouds. In the distance, beyond the woods, I can see a river, or perhaps it's the sea. It's shining in the moonlight. I look around me, and there seem to be rows of dark huts. It looks like a kind of village, a sort of primitive village. In fact, I know it's a village. But there doesn't seem to be anyone around.

'Then I'm walking across the grass towards the river. I know my way, because I feel I've been living on this strange island all my life. I feel that I am frightened, but at the same time I feel I have some hidden powers of my own, and that I am probably capable of overcoming my fear. I am frightened of the unknown – things that I don't understand.

'I reach the river and I stand on the beach. It is still very cold. I look across the water and I can see a big dark sailing ship anchored offshore. There is nothing in my dream which suggests that it's anything else but an ordinary sailing ship, but at the same time I am very frightened by it. It seems strange and unfamiliar, almost as though it's a flying saucer from another world.

'I stand on the beach for a long time, and then I see a small boat leave the sailing ship and start rowing towards the shore. I cannot see who is in the boat. I start running across the grass, back to the village, and then I go into one of the huts. The hut seems familiar. I know I have been there before. In fact, I can almost believe that it's *my* hut. There is an odd smell in it, like herbs or incense or something.

'I have a desperately urgent feeling that there is something I must do. I don't quite know what it is. But I must do it, whatever it is. It is something to do with the frightening people in the boat, something to do with this dark sailing ship. The fear seems to grow and grow inside me until I can hardly think. Something is going to come out of the ship which will have a terrible effect. There is something in that ship that is alien, something powerful and magical, and I am desperate about it. Then I wake up.'

Miss Tandy was screwing a handkerchief round and around in her fingers. Her voice was soft and light, but it carried a prickly kind of conviction that made me distinctly uneasy. I watched her as she spoke, and she seemed to believe that whatever she had dreamed about was something that had actually happened to her.

I took off my Green Bay Packers hat. It was a little incongruous, under the circumstances.

'Miss Tandy, that's a very odd dream. Is it always the same – in every detail?'

'Exactly. It's always the same. There is always this fear of what is coming out of the ship.'

'Hmm. And you say it's a *sailing* ship! Like a yacht, something like that?'

She shook her head. 'It's not a yacht. It's more like a galleon – one of those old-time galleons. You know, three masts and lots of rigging.'

I pulled my nose some more and thought hard. 'Is there anything about this ship which gives you a clue to what it is? Is there a name on it?'

'It's too far away. It's too dark.'

'Does it fly any flags?'

'There is a flag, but I couldn't describe it.'

I stood up and went over to my bookcase of occult paperbacks. I pulled out *Ten Thousand Dreams Interpreted* and a couple of others. I laid them out on the green baize table and looked up one or two references about islands and ships. They weren't helpful. Occult textbooks are almost invariably unhelpful, and often they're downright confusing. But that doesn't stop me from drawing a few dark and mysterious conclusions about my clients' nocturnal flights of fancy.

'Ships are usually connected with some kind of travel, or the arrival of news. In your case, the ship is dark, and frightening, which suggests to me that the news may not be good news. The island represents your feelings of isolation and fear, in fact the island represents *yourself*. Whatever this news may be, it is a direct threat to you, as a person.'

Karen Tandy nodded. I don't know why, but I felt really guilty handing her out all this bullshit. There was something genuinely defenceless and tense about her, and there she was with her dark brown bobbed hair and her pale impish face, so serious and lost, and I began to wonder if her dreams were really real.

'Miss Tandy,' I said. 'May I call you Karen?'

'Of course.

'I'm Harry. My grandmother calls me Henry, but no one else does.'

'It's a nice name.'

'Thank you. Look, listen, Karen, I'm going to be frank with you. I don't know why, but there's something about your case that doesn't strike the same kind of bells as the usual stuff I get. You know, old ladies trying to get in touch with their Pekinese dogs in the happy kennels in the sky, that kind of garbage. There's something about your dream that's — I don't know, *authentic*.'

This didn't reassure her at all. The last thing that people want to be told is that their fears are actually well founded. Even intelligent, educated people like to be comforted with the thought that their night-time visitations are all a cozy kind of bunkum. I mean, Jesus, if half the nightmares that people had were actually *real*, they'd go straight off their heads. Part of my job was soothing over my clients' terror, and telling them that the things they dream about were never going to happen.

'What do you mean, *authentic*?'

I handed her another cigarette. This time, when she lit it, her hands weren't quite so trembly.

'It's like this, Karen. Some people, even though they're not aware of it, have the potential power to be mediums. In other words, they're very receptive to all the occult buzzfuzz that's flying about in the atmosphere. A medium is like a radio, or a television set. Because of the way he or she is made, she's capable of picking up signals that other people can't, and she can interpret them into sound or pictures.'

'What signals?' She frowned. 'I don't understand.'

'There are all kinds of signals,' I said. 'You can't see a television signal, can you? Yet it's around you, all the time. This whole room is crowded with images and ghosts, pictures of David Brinkley and advertisements for Kellogg's Cornflakes. All you have to do to pick them up is have the right kind of receiver.'

Karen Tandy puffed smoke. 'You mean that my dream is

a signal? But what kind of a signal? And where could it come from? And why does it pick on me?'

I shook my head. 'I don't know why it's picked on you, and I don't know where it's from. It could have come from anywhere. There are authenticated reports of people in America having dreams that have given them detailed information about people in other countries far away. There was a farmer in Iowa who dreamed that he was drowning in a flood in Pakistan, and the same night there was a monsoon rain in Pakistan that killed four hundred people. The only way you can account for stuff like this is by thinking of thought waves as signals. The farmer picked up the signal, through his subconscious mind, from a Pakistani guy who was drowning. It's weird, I know, but it has happened.'

Karen Tandy looked at me appealingly. 'So how can I ever find out what my dream is really all about? Supposing it's a signal from someone, somewhere in the world, who needs help, and I can't find out who it is?'

'Well, if you're really interested in finding out, there's one way to do it,' I told her.

'Please – just tell me what to do. I really do want to know. I mean, I'm sure it's something to do with this – tumour thing, and I want to know what it is.'

I nodded. 'Okay, Karen, then this is what you do. Tonight, I want you to go to sleep as usual, and if you have the same dream over again, I want you to try and remember as many details – *factual* details – as you can. Look around the island and see if you can spot any landmarks. When you go down to the river, try and map out as much of the coastline as you can. If there's a bay or something, try and remember the shape of it. If there's anything across the river, any mountain or harbour or anything like that, fix it in your mind. Now there's one other thing that's very important; try and get a look at the flag on the sailing-ship. Memorize it. Then, the moment you wake up, note everything down in as much detail as you can, and make as many pictorial sketches as you can of everything you've seen. Then bring it to me.'

She stubbed out her cigarette. 'I have to be at the hospital by eight tomorrow morning.'

'Which hospital?'

'Sister of Jerusalem.'

'Well, look, because it's obviously important, I'll drop by the hospital and you can leave the notes for me in an envelope. How's that?'

'Mr Erskine – Harry, that's terrific. At last I really feel I'm getting down to something.'

I came over and took her hand in mine. She was cute, in her pixie kind of way, and if I hadn't been utterly professional and detached from my clients, and if she hadn't been going into hospital the next day, I think I would definitely have taken her for dinner, a friendly ride in my Cougar, and back to Erskine's occult emporium for a night of earthy activity.

'How much do I owe you?' she said, breaking the spell.

'Pay me next week,' I replied. It's always boosted the morale of people who were going into hospital if you asked them to pay you *after* their operation. It suddenly made them think that perhaps they were going to live, after all.

'Okay, Harry, thank you,' she said softly, and stood up to leave.

'You don't mind finding your own way out, do you?' I asked. I flapped my green gown around by way of explanation. 'The neighbours, you know. They think I'm a transvestite or something.'

Karen Tandy smiled, and said good night. I wondered how good it was really going to be. After she'd left, I sat down in my armchair and had a long think. There was something wrong with all this. Usually, when my clients came fluttering in to tell me their dreams, they were standard technicolour epics of frustrated sex and erotic embarrassment, like going to a cocktail party with the Vaunderbilts and finding your knickers round your ankles. There were dreams of flying and dreams of eating, and dreams of accidents and nameless fears but none of the dreams had ever had the uncanny photographic clarity, and the same totally logical sequence, as the dream of Karen Tandy.

I picked up the telephone and dialled. It rang for a couple of minutes before it was answered.

'Hello?' said an elderly voice. 'Who is this?'

'Mrs Karmann, this is Harry Erskine. I'm sorry to trouble you so late.'

'Why, Mr *Erskine*. How nice to hear your voice. I was in the tub, you know, but I'm all snuggled up in my bath-towel now.'

'Oh, I'm sorry. Mrs Karmann, do you mind if I ask you a question?'

The old dear giggled. 'As long as it's not too *personal*, Mr Erskine.'

'I'm afraid not, Mrs Karmann. Listen, Mrs Karmann, do you recall a dream you told me about, two or three months ago?'

'Which one was it, Mr Erksine? The one about my husband?'

'That's right. The one about your husband asking you for help.'

'Well, now, let me see,' said Mrs Karmann. 'If I remember it rightly, I was standing by the seaside, and it was the middle of the night, and it was awfully cold. I remember thinking I ought to have put my wrap on before I'd come out. Then I heard my husband whispering to me. He always whispers, you know. He never comes out loud and shouts in my ear. He was whispering something I didn't understand at all, but I was sure he was aking for *help*'

I felt distinctly strange and worried. I don't mind messing around with the occult when it behaves itself, but when it starts acting up, then I start getting a little bit of the creeps.

'Mrs Karmann,' I said. 'Do you recall seeing anything else in your dream, apart from a seashore? Was there a ship or a boat out there? Did you see any huts, or a village?'

'I can't recall there was anything else,' replied Mrs Karmann. 'Is there any particular reason you want to know?'

'It's just some article I'm writing on dreams for a magazine, Mrs Karmann. Nothing important. I just thought I'd like to include one or two of your dreams, since they've always been very interesting.'

I could almost see the old lady fluttering her eyelashes. 'Why, Mr Erskine, that's *awfully* nice of you to say so.'

'Oh, one thing more, Mrs Karmann. And this is important.'

'Yes, Mr Erskine?'

'Don't tell anyone else about this conversation. Nobody else at all. Do you understand me?'

She let out breath, as though the last thing in the whole world that would ever occur to her would be to gossip.

'Not a *whisper*, Mr Erskine, I swear.'

'Thank you, Mrs Karmann. You've been a terrific help,' I said, and I laid down the phone more slowly and carefully than I've ever done in my life.

Was it possible for two people to have identical dreams? If it was, then maybe all this bunk about signals from beyond could be real. Maybe both Karen Tandy and her aunt Mrs Karmann were capable of picking up a message from *out there* – from out of the night, and playing it through in their minds.

I didn't take any notice of the fact that Mrs Karmann claimed it was her husband trying to get in touch with her. All elderly widows thought their husbands were floating around in the ether, anxiously trying to tell them something of vital importance, whereas what their phantom partners were probably doing out there in spirit-land was playing golf, squeezing the ghostly tits of nubile young girls, and enjoying a few years of peace and quiet before their erstwhile wives came up to join them.

What *I* thought was that the same person was trying to get in touch with both of them, trying to communicate some nameless fear that had gripped her. I guessed it was probably a woman, but you couldn't really tell with spirits. They were supposed to be more or less sexless, and I guess it must be hard trying to make love to a luscious spirit lady with nothing more substantial than an ectoplasmic penis.

I was sitting in my flat thinking all these irreverent thoughts when I had the oddest sensation that someone was standing behind me, just out of my line of vision. I didn't want to turn around, because that would have been an admission of ridiculous fear, but all the same there was an itching feeling in the middle of my back, and I couldn't help casting my eyes sideways to see if there were any unaccustomed shadows on the wall.

Eventually, I stood up, and threw a rapid glance backwards. Of course, there was nothing there. But I couldn't help thinking that *something* or *somebody* had been – somebody dark and monkish and silent. I whistled rather loudly and went to pour myself three or four fingers of Scotch. If there was one kind of spirit of which I thoroughly approved, it was this. The sharp bite of malt and barley brought me down to earth in very rapid order.

I decided to cast the Tarot cards, to see what they had to say about all this. Now, out of all the mumbo-jumbo of clairvoyance and spiritualism, I have a certain respect for the Tarot, in spite of myself. I don't *want* to believe in it, but it has a peculiar knack of telling you exactly what kind of state you're in, no matter how hard you're trying to hide it. And each card had an odd feeling about it, as though it's a momentary picture from a dream you can never quite recall.

I shuffled the cards and laid them out on the green baize table. I use the Celtic cross arrangement of ten cards because it's the easiest. 'This crosses you, this crowns you, this is beneath you, this is behind you . . .'

I asked the Tarot one simple question, and I obeyed all the rules and kept it firmly in front of my mind. The question was: '*Who is talking to Karen Tandy from beyond?*'

As I laid out the cards, one by one, I couldn't help frowning. I had never had such a peculiar reading in my life. Some Tarot cards hardly ever come up, and when they do, they strike you straight away because they're so unfamiliar. Most people's readings are full of minor litigation cards, or cards that show anxiety about money, or arguments in the home – all the lesser cards in the suits of cups and wands and pentacles. You very seldom see cards of terrible disasters, like The Tower, which shows tiny people hurled out of a castle by a jagged flash of lightning, and I had never once turned up Death.

But Death came up, in his black armour, on his red-eyed black horse, with bishops and children bowing in front of him. And so did the Devil, with his hostile hairy glare, his

31

ram's horns, and naked people chained to his throne. And so did the Magician, reversed. This way round, the Magician's card signified a physician or magus, mental disease and disquiet.

I sat staring at the cards for almost half an hour. The Magician? What the hell did that mean? Did it mean that Karen Tandy was mentally disordered? Maybe it did. Perhaps that tumour on the neck had affected her brain. The trouble with these damned cards was that they were never specific enough. They gave you four or five varying interpretations, and you had to make your own mind up.

The Magician? I shuffled the cards again, and used the Magician card as my question. To do that, I had to place it in the centre of the table, cover it over with another card, and lay out the Celtic cross all over again. The cards would then give me a more detailed explanation of what the Magician was all about.

Nine cards went down, and then I turned up the tenth. I had a very weird sensation in the bottom of my stomach, and I started to feel that someone was watching me again. This couldn't be possible. The tenth card was the Magician, too.

I lifted the card that covered my question card, and under there was Death. Perhaps I'd made a mistake. All the same, I was pretty sure I'd laid the Magician down first. I took up all the cards again, and placed the Magician firmly down there on the table, and covered it over with the two of wands, and went on putting down cards until I came to the last one.

There was nothing on it at all. It was blank.

I didn't believe in all this fortune-telling stuff, but I definitely got the feeling that someone out there was telling me loudly and firmly to mind my own business.

I looked at my watch. It was midnight. A good time for ghosts and spirits and a good time to be getting to bed. Tomorrow, I was definitely going to take a look at what Karen Tandy had scribbled down in her envelope.

# CHAPTER TWO

# INTO THE DARK

The next morning, Saturday, an orange sun showed up at around half past ten and the snowy streets started to turn into heaps of brown slush. It was still freezing cold, and my Cougar stalled twice on the way to the Sisters of Jerusalem Hospital. Passers-by went splashing along the filthy sidewalks in coats and mufflers, faceless black figures out of a winter's dream.

I parked right outside the hospital and went into the reception hall. It was warm and ritzy in there, with thick carpet and potted palms, and the murmur of conversation. It seemed more like a holiday resort than a home for the sick. I was greeted at the counter by a smart young lady with a white starched uniform and white starched teeth.

'Can I help you?'

'Yes, I believe you can. There was supposed to be an envelope left here for me this morning. My name's Erskine, Harry Erskine.'

'Just a moment, please.'

She sorted through a pile of letters and postcards, and eventually came back with a small white envelope.

'The Incredible Erskine?' she read, with one eyebrow lifted.

I coughed in embarrassment. 'Just a nickname. You know how it is.'

'Do you have some identification, sir?'

I shuffled through my pockets. My driver's licence was at home, and so were my credit cards. Eventually I came across one of my calling cards, and showed it to her. Written across it was: 'The Incredible Erskine. Fortunes told, forecasts interpreted, dreams delved.'

'I guess you must be him all right,' she smiled, and handed over the letter.

I waited until I reached my flat before I examined the envelope. I laid it on the table and inspected it closely. Just the sort of handwriting you would expect from a cultivated girl like Karen Tandy – firm, sweeping and bold. I particularly liked the way she'd written *Incredible*. I found a pair of nail-scissors in the table drawer and cut along the top of the envelope. Inside were three or four sheets of lined paper, that looked as though they'd been torn from a secretary's notepad. There was a short letter with them, in Karen Tandy's script:

'Dear Mr Erskine,

I had the dream again last night, much more vivid than before. I have tried to remember every detail, and two things were very striking. The coastline had a particular shape which I have sketched down here. I have also sketched the sailing-ship, and as much of its flag as I can remember.

The feeling of *fear* was also very much stronger, and the sense of needing to *escape* was extremely powerful.

As soon as I have recovered from the operation, I will call you to see what you think.

Your friend, Karen Tandy.'

I opened up the scraps of note-paper and peered at them closely. The improvized map of the coastline was distinctly unhelpful. It was little more than a squiggly line that could have been anywhere in the world. But the drawing of the ship was more interesting. It was quite detailed, and the flag was good, too. There were bound to be books on sailing-ships in the library and books of flags, as well, so there was a chance that I could discover which ship this actually was.

If it *was* a real ship at all, and wasn't just a figment of Karen Tandy's tumour-ridden imagination.

I sat there for quite a while, pondering over the strange case of 'my friend, Karen Tandy'. I was eager to go and check on the ship, but it was nearly half past eleven, and Mrs Herz was due – another dear old lady with more money than sense. Mrs Herz's special interest was in knowing whether

34

she was going to have any trouble with her hundreds of relations, all of whom were mentioned in her will. After every session with me, she went to her lawyer and altered everyone's legacy. Her lawyer made so much money out of these codicils and amendments that last Christmas he had sent me a crate of Black Label Johnnie Walker. After all, he and I were in much the same kind of business.

At eleven-thirty sharp there was a ring at the door. I hung up my jacket in the closet, took down my long green robe, stuck my hat on top of my head, and prepared to receive Mrs Herz in my usual mystical manner.

'Come in, Mrs Herz. It's a fine morning for everything occult.'

Mrs Herz must have been all of seventy-five. She was pallid and wrinkled with hands like chicken's claws, and spectacles that magnified her eyes like oysters swimming in goldfish bowls. She came trembling in on her stick, smelling of mothballs and lavender, and she sat herself down in my armchair with a frail, reedy sigh.

'How are you, Mrs Herz?' I asked her cheerily, rubbing my hands. 'How are the dreams?'

She said nothing at all, so I simply shrugged and went to collect the Tarot cards together. As I shuffled them, I tried to find the blank card that I had turned up last night, but there didn't seem to be any sign of it. I could have been mistaken of course, or overtired, but I wasn't entirely convinced of that. In spite of my job, I'm not given to mystical experiences. I laid the cards out on the table, and invited Mrs Herz to think of a question she would like to ask them.

'It's a long time since we checked up on your nephew Stanley,' I reminded her. 'How about a peek at the comings and goings of that little household? Or how about your step-sister Agnes?'

She didn't answer. She didn't even look at me. She seemed to be staring over into a corner of the room, lost in a dream of her own.

'Mrs Herz?' I said, standing up. 'Mrs Herz, I've laid the cards out for you.'

35

I went over and bent down to look in her face. She seemed all right. She was breathing, at least. The last thing I wanted was an old lady giving up the ghost when I was in the middle of telling her fortune. The publicity would be ruinous. Or then again, maybe it wouldn't.

I took her old, reptilian hands in mine and said gently: 'Mrs Herz? Are you feeling all right? Can I get you a glass of brandy?'

Her eyes floated eerily around in her Coke-bottle glasses. She seemed to be looking in my direction, but at the same time she didn't focus on me at all. It was almost as though she were looking *through* me, or behind me. I couldn't help turning around to see if there was somebody else in the room.

'Mrs Herz,' I said again. 'Do you want one of your pills, Mrs Herz? Can you hear me, Mrs Herz?'

A thin, sibilant whisper dribbled out from between her withered lips. I had the feeling she was trying to say something, but I couldn't work it out at all. The oil lamp started flickering and guttering, and it was hard to make out whether the moving shadows across her face were strange expressions or not.

'Booooo . . .' she said faintly.

'Mrs Herz,' I snapped. 'If this is some kind of game, you'd better stop. You've got me worried here. Mrs Herz, if you don't get yourself together at once I'm going to call an ambulance. Do you understand me, Mrs Herz?'

'Booo . . .' she whispered again. Her hands started shaking, and her large emerald ring vibrated against the arm of the chair. Her eyes were rolling around, and her jaw seemed to be stuck wide open. I could see her pale slimy tongue, and her $4,000 bridgework.

'Okay,' I said. 'That's it. I'm calling an ambulance, Mrs Herz. Look, here I am going to the telephone. I'm dialling the number, Mrs Herz. It's ringing.'

Suddenly the old lady stood up. She grabbed for her stick, missed it, and it clattered on to the floor. She stood swaying and shuffling on the carpet, as though she were dancing in time to some song that I couldn't hear. The operator said:

'Yes, can I help you?' but I put the phone down and went across to my hopping, waltzing old client.

I tried to put my arm around her, but she flapped me away with one of her scaly paws. She jogged and danced, muttering and mumbling all the time, and I just didn't know what the hell to do with her. She must be having some kind of fit, but I'd never seen a fit where the sufferer does a one-woman conga round the floor.

'Booo . . .' she whispered again.

I danced around her, trying to keep up with her scuffly little waltz. 'What do you mean, "boo"?' I asked her. 'Mrs Herz, will you please sit down and relax, and tell me what the hell's going on?'

As abruptly as she had started to dance, she stopped. The energy seemed to fall out of her like an elevator sinking to floor-level, foyer and street. She reached out for something to support her, and I had to grab her arm to stop her from pitching over. I gently laid her stiff old body back into the armchair, and knelt down beside her.

'Mrs Herz, I don't like to bully my clients, but I do think you ought to have some medical attention. Now, don't you agree that would be sensible?'

She stared at me blindly, and her mouth stretched open again. I admit I had to look away. The *outsides* of old ladies are okay, but I'm really not too keen on their insides.

'Boot,' she whispered. 'Boot.'

'Boot?' I asked her. 'What the hell have *boots* got to do with anything?'

'Boot,' she quivered, much more shrilly now. '*Boot!* BOOOTTTTT!!'

'My God,' I said. 'Mrs Herz, just you calm down and I'll fetch an ambulance straight away. Now, don't move, Mrs Herz, its perfectly all right. You're going to be fine, just fine.'

I got up and went over to the telephone and dialled the emergency service. Mrs Herz was shaking and trembling and rabbiting on about 'boot, boot' and they seemed to take half an hour to answer.

'*Can I help you?*' said the operator, at last.

'You certainly can. Look, I need an ambulance straight

37

away. I have an old lady here who's having some kind of a fit. She's as rich as they come, so tell the ambulance crew they don't have to make any detours through the Bronx before they get here. Please hurry. I think she's going to die or something.'

I gave my address and telephone number, and then turned back to Mrs Herz. She seemed to have stopped twitching for the moment, and she was sitting there quiet and strange as though she was thinking.

'Mrs Herz . . .' I said.

She turned towards me. Her face was old and fixed and rigid. Her watery eyes stared right into mine.

'De boot, mijnheer,' she said gruffly. 'De boot.'

'Mrs Herz, look, please, you don't have to worry. The ambulance is on its way. Just sit there and keep calm.'

Mrs Herz gripped the arm of the chair and got to her feet. She had trouble standing straight, as though she were walking on ice. But then she pulled herself erect, and stood there with her arms hanging down by her side, taller and firmer than I'd ever seen her stand before.

'Mrs Herz, I think you'd better . . .'

But she ignored me, and started to glide across the carpet. I'd never seen anybody walk that way before. Her feet seemed to skate silently over the floor as if she wasn't really touching it at all. She slid quietly over to the door, and opened it.

'It really would be better if you waited,' I said lamely. To tell you the truth, I was getting the creeps with all this, and I didn't know what to say to her at all. She didn't seem to hear me, or if she did, she wasn't taking any notice.

'De Boot,' she said again, in a harsh voice. And then she glided out of the door and into the corridor.

Of course, I went after her. But what I saw next was so sudden and weird that I almost wished I hadn't. One second she was just outside the door, and I was reaching out my hand to take her arm, and then she was sliding away down the long bright corridor, as quickly as if she was running. But she wasn't running at all. She was rushing away from me *without even moving her legs.*

'Mrs Herz!' I called, but my voice went strangled and strange. I felt a huge dark surge of fright inside me, like seeing a white face at the window in the middle of the night.

She turned, once, at the end of the corridor. She was standing at the head of the stairs. She seemed to be trying to beckon, or lift her arm — more as if she were fighting something off than trying to call me to help her. Then she disappeared down the stairs, and I heard her stiff old body falling and bumping from step to step.

I pelted down to the end of the corridor. Doors were opening all the way along, and anxious and curious faces were peering out.

I looked down the stairs. Mrs Herz was lying there, all twisted up, with her legs at peculiar angles. I rushed down and knelt beside her and felt her stick-like wrist. Nothing, no pulse at all. I lifted her head, and a long slide of glutinous blood came pouring out of her mouth.

'Is she okay?' said one of my neighbours, from the top of the stairs. 'What happened?'

'She fell,' I told him. 'She's seventy-five. She's not too good on her feet. I think she's dead. I called an ambulance already.'

'Oh, God,' said a woman. 'I can't stand anything dead.'

I stood up, tearing my long green gown. I just couldn't believe any of this, and I felt as if I'd wake up in a moment, and it would still be early morning, and I'd be lying in bed in my turquoise silk pyjamas. I looked down at Mrs Herz, wrinkled and old and extinct, like a pale balloon that's leaked itself to death, and the sick started rising in my throat.

Lieutenant Marino of the Homicide Squad was most understanding. It turned out that Mrs Herz had left me something in her will, but it wasn't enough for me to have pushed her down the stairs.

The detective sat upright in my armchair, in his stiff black raincoat, with his black brush-cut hair sticking up at all angles, trying to read from a grubby scrap of paper.

'It says here that you're entitled to a pair of Victorian

vases,' he sniffed. 'We're having someone check on the value right now, but you don't look the kind of guy who'd knock an old lady off for a vase.'

I shrugged. 'Old ladies like her are my bread-and-butter. You don't go pushing your bread-and-butter down the stairs.'

Lieutenant Marino looked up. He had a wide, squashed face, like an opera singer who's fallen on hard times. He scratched his spiky hair thoughtfully and cast his eyes around the room.

'Some kind of fortune-teller, aren't you?'

'That's right. Tarot cards, tea-leaves, that kind of stuff. Most of my clients are elderly ladies like Mrs Herz.'

He bit his lip and nodded. 'Sure. You say she was acting unwell the whole time she was here?'

'Yes, I mean I thought there was something wrong from the moment she came in. She's pretty old and infirm, but she usually manages to chat for a while, and tell me how she's getting on. But this time she came in and sat down and never said a word.'

Lieutenant Marino stared at his piece of paper. 'Did you get around to telling her fortune? What I mean is, was there any reason she might have killed herself? Any bad news in the tea-leaves?'

'Not a chance. I didn't even lay the cards out. She just came in and sat down and started rambling on about boots.'

'Boots? What do you mean by that?'

'I don't know. She kept on saying "boot, boot". Don't ask me.'

'Boot?' frowned Lieutenant Marino. 'What kind of way did she say it? Did it sound like a name? Did it sound like she was trying to tell you about a guy named Boot?'

I thought hard, tugging my nose. 'I don't think so. I mean, it didn't *sound* like a name. But she seemed very worried about it.'

Lieutenant Marino looked interested. 'Worried? How do you mean?'

'Well, it's hard to say, really. She came in, sat down, and started all this "boot" stuff, and then she went out of the door and ran off up the corridor. I tried to stop her, but she was much too quick for me. She waved her arms around a bit, and then fell straight down the stairs.'

The detective made a couple of notes. Then he said: 'Ran?'

I spread my arms open. 'Don't ask me how, because I don't understand it myself. But she ran up the corridor like a girl of fifteen.'

Lieutenant Marino frowned. 'Mr Erskine, the dead woman was seventy-five years old. She walked with a stick. And you're trying to tell me she *ran* up the corridor? *Ran?*'

'That's what I said.'

'Come on, now, Mr Erskine – don't you think you're letting your imagination run a little wild? I don't believe you killed her, but I certainly don't believe she *ran*.'

I looked down at the floor. I remembered the way that Mrs Herz had skated out of the room, and the way that she'd dwindled away down the corridor as though she were running on rails.

'Well, to be truthful, she didn't exactly *run*,' I told him.

'So what did she do?' asked Lieutenant Marino patiently. 'Walked, maybe? Shuffled?'

'No, she didn't walk, and she didn't shuffle. She *slid*.'

Lieutenant Marino was just about to make a note of that, but his pen stopped an eighth of an inch from his paper. He grunted, grinned, and then tucked the paper away in his coat. He stood up, and came over to me with an indulgent smile on his face.

'Listen, Mr Erskine, it's always a shock when somebody dies. It tends to play tricks on your mind. You should know that, you're in the business. Maybe you just thought you saw something a different way from the way it actually happened.'

'Yes,' I said dumbly. 'It could be.'

He laid a podgy hand on my shoulder, and gave me a friendly squeeze.

'There's going to be a post-mortem examination to establish the cause of death, but I doubt if it will go any further than that. I might have to send someone round again to ask you one or two more questions, but otherwise you're in the clear. I'd ask you not to leave the city for a day or two, but you mustn't think you're under arrest, or anything like that.'

I nodded. 'Okay, lieutenant. I understand. Thank you for coming round so quickly.'

'It's a pleasure. I'm sorry your client – you know, departed for the spirit-world like that.'

I managed a wan little grin. 'I'm sure she'll be in touch,' I said. 'You can't keep a good spirit down.'

I'm sure that Lieutenant Marino thought I was stark, staring mad. He pulled his little black hat over his hedge-like hair, and made for the door.

'So long then, Mr Erskine.'

After he'd gone, I sat down and thought for a while. Then I picked up the telephone and dialled the Sisters of Jerusalem Hospital.

'Hello,' I said. 'I'm inquiring about a patient of yours. Miss Karen Tandy. She came in this morning for an operation.'

'Hold on, please. Are you a relative?'

'Oh, yes,' I lied. 'I'm her uncle. I just got into town and heard she was sick.'

'Just a moment, please.'

I drummed my fingers on the table while I waited. The faint sounds of the hospital came down the line, and I could hear someone paging *Dr Hughes, please, Dr Hughes*. After a minute or so, another voice said: 'Hold on, please,' and I was connected through to another lot of noises.

Eventually, a nasal woman said: 'Can I help you? I understand you're inquiring about Miss Karen Tandy.'

'That's right. I'm her uncle. I heard she had an operation this morning and I just wanted to check she was okay.'

'Well, I'm sorry, sir, but Dr Hughes tells me there's been a little complication. Miss Tandy is still under sedation, and we're having another specialist come in to look at her.'

'Complications?' I said. 'What kind of complications?'

'I'm sorry, sir, but I can't tell you that over the phone. If you want to call in, I could make an appointment for you with Dr Hughes.'

'Hmm,' I said. 'No, don't worry. Maybe I could call you tomorrow to check how she is.'

'Okay, sir. You're welcome.'

I put down the phone. Maybe I shouldn't be worrying, but I was. The strange way in which the cards had behaved last night, and that unnerving incident with Mrs Herz, not to mention the odd dreams of Karen Tandy and her aunt – everything was making me feel queasy and suspicious. Suppose there really *was* something out there, something spiritual and powerful and unfriendly?

I went back to the green-baize table and took out Karen Tandy's letter and drawings. The coastline, the ship and the flag. Three sketchy pictures from the shores of the night. Three imaginary clues to a problem that might not even exist. I tucked them in my pocket, picked up my car keys, and went off to check them out at the library.

It was almost closing-time when I reached the library, and wrestled my Cougar into a tiny parking-space on a pile of brown slush. The sky was a dark coppery green, which meant there was more snow on the way, and a bitter wind sliced through my herringbone overcoat. I locked the car and trudged through ankle-deep drifts to the warm wooden library doors.

The girl behind the desk looked more like a retired madame than a librarian. She wore a tight red cardigan and black piled-up hair, and her teeth would have fitted a horse.

'I'm looking for ships,' I told her, kicking the melting snow off my shoes.

'Why don't you try the docks?' she grinned. 'We only have books here.'

'Ha ha,' I replied coldly. 'Now will you tell me where the ships are?'

'Upstairs, fifth or sixth shelf along. Under SH for keep quiet.'

I stared at her in amazement. 'Did you ever think of going into vaudeville?' I asked.

'Vaudeville's dead,' she snapped.

'So are your jokes,' I told her, and went in search of ships.

You know something, I never realized how many different

43

kinds of ship there are. I thought there were only about two or three varieties – big ones, little ones and aircraft carriers. But by the time I'd skimmed through fifteen books on maritime engineering, I began to appreciate the size of my task. There were dhows and xebecs, barques and brigantines, frigates and corvettes and destroyers and jolly-boats and dinghies and coracles and barges and tugs and you name it. About half of them looked exactly like Karen Tandy's funny little sketch.

I came across the right one almost by accident. I was heaving out a heap of six or seven books, when I dropped the lot with a clatter on the floor. An old guy in glasses who was studying a huge tome on seals (see under SE) turned around and glared me into the ground.

'I'm sorry,' I said apologetically, and gathered up all the fallen books. And there it was, right under my nose. The identical ship. To me, all old sailing ships were 'galleons', and pretty much alike, but there was something distinctive about the shape of this hull and the way the masts were arranged. It was definitely the ship of Karen Tandy's dreams.

The caption underneath the picture said *Dutch Man of War, circa 1650.*

The odd prickly feeling went up the back of my neck. *Dutch.* And what was it that old Mrs Herz had muttered, back there in my flat? *De boot, mijnheer, de boot.*

I took the ship book under my arm and went downstairs to the foreign language section. I lifted out an English-Dutch dictionary, flicked through the pages, and there it was. *De boot,* the ship.

Now I'm as reasonable and logical as the next man, but this was more than a coincidence. Karen Tandy had been having nightmares about a Dutch ship from the seventeenth century, and then old Mrs Herz had started having hallucinations or God knows what about just the same thing. *How* and *why* were questions that I just couldn't answer, but it seemed to me that if Mrs Herz had been killed by her visitation, then the same thing could happen to Karen Tandy.

I went back to the desk and checked out the book on ships. The old whore with the horse-like teeth and the black hair gave me a sardonic grin, and that didn't exactly make me feel any better. A woman like that was enough to give you nightmares on her own, without worrying about mysterious sailing boats from another century.

'Enjoy your reading,' she grinned, and I pulled a face at her.

Outside, I found a phone booth, but I had to wait in the freezing wind and snow while a short fat woman called her ailing sister in Minnesota. It was one of those conversations that chases its own tail, and just when you think they're going to wrap it up, they start all over. In the end, I had to bang on the glass, and the woman glared at me, but at least she finished her epic dialogue.

I got into the phone booth and thumbed in my dime. I dialled the Sisters of Jerusalem Hospital, and asked for Dr Hughes. I had to hang on for four or five minutes, stamping the circulation back into my feet, and at last the doctor answered.

'Dr Hughes here, can I help you?'

'You don't know me, Dr Hughes,' I said. 'My name is Harry Erskine and I'm a clairvoyant.'

'A what?'

'A clairvoyant. You know, fortunes told, that kind of stuff.'

'Well, I'm sorry Mr Erskine, but—'

'No, please,' I interrupted. 'Just listen for one minute. Yesterday I had a visit from a patient of yours, a girl named Karen Tandy.'

'Oh, really?'

'Dr Hughes, Miss Tandy told me that ever since she had first felt that tumour of hers, she'd been having recurrent nightmares.'

'That's not uncommon,' said Dr Hughes impatiently. 'Many of my patients are subconsciously disturbed by their conditions.'

'But there's more to it than that, Dr Hughes. The nightmare was very detailed and very specific, and she dreamed about a ship. It wasn't just any old ship, either. She made me a drawing of it, and it turned out to be a very particular ship. A Dutch man of war, dated about 1650.'

'Mr Erskine,' said Dr Hughes. 'I'm a very busy man, and I don't know whether I can—'

'Please, Dr Hughes, just listen,' I asked him. 'This morning another client of mine came to visit me, and she started talking in Dutch about a ship. She was the kind of woman who wouldn't have known a Dutchman if he'd come up wearing clogs and given her a bunch of tulips. She got very upset and hysterical, and then she had an accident.'

'What kind of accident?'

'Well, she fell downstairs. She was seventy-five years old, and it killed her.'

There was a silence.

'Dr Hughes?' I said. 'Are you still there?'

'Yes, I'm still here. Listen, Mr Erskine, why are you telling me all this?'

'Because I think it's relevant to Karen Tandy, Dr Hughes. I was told this morning that she had some kind of complications. This dream has already killed one of my clients. I'm worried in case the same thing happens again.'

Another silence, longer this time.

Finally, Dr Hughes said: 'Mr Erskine, this is very irregular. I'm not saying for one moment that I understand what you're trying to get at, but you seem to have some kind of idea about my patient's condition. Do you think I could persuade you to come up to the hospital and talk to me about it? There may be nothing in it, but to tell you the truth we're at a complete impasse with Karen Tandy, and anything, no matter how small, could help us understand what's wrong with her.'

'Now you're talking,' I told him. 'Give me fifteen minutes, and I'll be right there. Should I just ask for you?'

'That's right,' said Dr Hughes tiredly. 'Just ask for me.'

By the time I arrived, the slush was freezing up again, and the streets were slidey and treacherous. I parked in the basement of the hospital, and took the elevator up to the recep-

46

tion desk. The girl with the Colgate smile said: 'Well hello –
it's the Incredible Erskine, isn't it?'

'It certainly is,' I told her. 'I have an appointment with Dr
Hughes.'

She buzzed his office, and then directed me to the eighteenth floor. I rose in the warm, hushed elevator, and
emerged into a thick-carpeted corridor. A shingle above the
door in front of me read *Dr J. H. Hughes*, and I knocked.

Dr Hughes was a small, weary man who looked as though
he needed a week-end in the mountains.

'Mr Erskine?' he said, limply shaking my hand. 'Take a
seat. Coffee? Or I have something stronger if you prefer it.'

'Coffee is terrific.'

He bleeped his secretary to fetch us drinks, and then he sat
back in his big black swivel armchair and laced his hands
behind his head.

'I've been dealing with tumours for a good many years
now, Mr Erskine, and I've seen them all. I'm supposed to be
an expert in my field. But I can tell you straight out that I've
never seen a case like Karen Tandy's, and I'm frankly bewildered by it.'

I lit a cigarette. 'What's so special about it?'

'The tumour isn't the normal kind of tumour. Without
going into too much grisly detail, it doesn't have any of the
usual characteristics of tumorous tissue. What she has there
is a fast-growing swelling made of both skin and bone. In
some ways, you could almost describe the tumour as being
like a foetus.'

'You mean – a baby? You mean she's having a *baby* – in
her *neck*? I don't understand you.'

Dr Hughes shrugged. 'Neither do I, Mr Erskine. There
are thousands of recorded cases of foetuses growing in the
wrong place. In the fallopian tube for example, or in various
kinds of annexations of the womb. But there is no precedent for any sort of foetus growing in the neck area, and
there is certainly no precedent for any sort of foetus growing
as fast as this one.'

'Didn't you operate on her this morning? I thought you
were going to remove it.'

Dr Hughes shook his head. 'That was the intention. We had her on the operating table, and everything was lined up for its removal. But as soon as the surgeon, Dr Snaith, started making an incision, her pulse-rate and respiration weakened so drastically that we had to stop. Another two or three minutes and she would have died. We had to satisfy ourselves with more X-rays.'

'Was there any reason for this?' I asked him. 'I mean, why did she get so sick?'

'I don't know,' said Dr Hughes. 'I'm having a series of tests run on her right now, which will maybe give us the answer. But I've never come across anything like it before, and I'm as mystified as anyone else.'

Dr Hughes' secretary brought us in a couple of cups of coffee and some biscuits. We sipped in silence for a while, and then I asked Dr Hughes the 64,000 dollar question.

'Dr Hughes,' I said. 'Do you believe in black magic?'

He stared at me thoughtfully.

'No,' he said. 'I don't.'

'I don't either,' I replied. 'But there's something about this whole business that strikes me as completely weird. You see, Karen Tandy's aunt is also a client of mine, and she has had the same kind of dream as Karen. Not so detailed, not so frightening – but definitely the same kind of dream.'

'Well?' asked Dr Hughes. 'What does that suggest to you – as a clairvoyant?'

I looked at the floor. 'I'll confess to you here and now, Dr Hughes, that I'm not a serious clairvoyant. It's my living, if you know what I mean. Usually I'm pretty sceptical about spirits and the occult. But it does seem to me that there's some kind of *outside influence* causing Karen Tandy's condition. In other words, something is making her dream these dreams, and maybe it's the same thing that's affecting her tumour and her health.'

Dr Hughes was suspicious. 'Are you trying to tell me she's possessed? Like *The Exorcist* or something?'

'No, I don't think so. I don't believe in that kind of demon. But I do believe that one person can dominate another, through the mind. And I think that somebody or someone

48

is dominating Karen Tandy. Somebody is transmitting a mental signal to her, a signal that's powerful enough to make her ill.'

'But what about her aunt? And this old lady client of yours – the one who fell down the stairs this morning?'

I shook my head. 'I don't think that this *somebody* really meant to harm them. But it's just like any powerful signal that's sent over a considerable distance – any receiver that happens to be in the area it's being sent tends to pick it up, too. Mrs Karmann and Mrs Herz were close to Karen Tandy, or to places where she'd been, and they picked up the backwash from the main transmission.'

Dr Hughes rubbed his eyes, and then looked at me narrowly. 'All right – supposing someone is sending a signal to Karen Tandy, with the intention of making her ill. Who is it, and why are they doing it?'

'Your guess is as good as mine. But don't you think it might do some good if we talk to Karen herself?'

Dr Hughes spread his hands. 'She's in pretty bad shape. Her parents are flying in this evening, in case we can't pull her round. But I guess it wouldn't affect her chances if we tried.'

He lifted the phone and spoke to his secretary. In a few minutes, she bleeped back and said she'd made arrangements for us to visit Karen.

'I'm afraid you'll have to wear a surgical mask, Mr Erskine,' said Dr Hughes. 'She's quite weak, and we don't want any more infections getting into her system.'

'That's okay by me.'

We went down to the tenth floor, and Dr Hughes showed me into a dressing-room. As we tied on green surgical robes and masks, he explained that he would have to ask me to leave if her condition worsened even slightly.

'I'm only letting you see her because you have a theory, Mr Erskine, and anybody with a theory could help us. But I warn you that this is all very unofficial, and I don't want to have to explain to anyone why you're here.'

'I get you,' I said, and followed him down the corridor to Karen Tandy's room.

It was a big corner room, with a view of the snowy night on two sides. The walls were pale hospital green, and there were no flowers or decorations, except for a small picture of an autumn day in New Hampshire. Karen Tandy's bed was surrounded with surgical equipment, and there was a clear drip feed going into her right arm. She had her eyes closed, and she looked as white and wan as the pillow she was lying on. There were dark umber circles around her eyes, and I could hardly recognize her as the girl who had come into my apartment the previous night.

But it was the tumour that was the most startling. It had swollen and grown around her neck, pale and fat and threaded with veins. It must have been twice the size it was the night before, and it was almost touching her shoulders at the back. I looked across at Dr Hughes and he simply shook his head.

I pulled up a chair to her bedside and laid my hand on her arm. She felt very cold. She stirred a little and her eyes opened slightly.

'Karen?' I said softly. 'It's me – Harry Erskine.'

'Hello,' she whispered. 'Hello, Harry Erskine.'

I leaned closer. 'Karen,' I said. 'I've found the ship. I went to the library and looked it up and it was there.'

Her eyes flickered towards me.

'You've – found it?'

'It's a Dutch ship, Karen. It was built around 1650.'

'Dutch?' she said weakly. 'I don't know what it could be.'

'Are you sure, Karen? Are you sure you haven't ever come across it before?'

She tried to shake her head, but the distended tumour prevented her. It bulged from the back of her neck like an awful pallid fruit.

Dr Hughes laid his hand on my shoulder. 'I don't think we're getting very far, Mr Erskine. Maybe we just ought to leave it.'

I grasped Karen's wrist more firmly.

'Karen,' I said. 'What about *de boot*? What about *de boot, mijnheer*?'

'The – what?' she whispered.

'*De boot*, Karen, *de boot*.'

She closed her eyes, and I thought she'd gone back to sleep again, but then something seemed to shift and stir on the bed. The bulging white tumour suddenly *wriggled*, as though there was something alive inside it.

'Oh, Christ,' said Dr Hughes. 'Mr Erskine, you'd better—'

'Aaaahhh,' groaned Karen. 'Aaaahhhhh.'

Her fingers clutched the sheets, and she tried to toss her head. The tumour squirmed and wriggled some more, as if it was clutching the back of her head, and squeezing it.

'AAAAAAAAAAAAAAHHHHHH!' she screamed. 'DE-BOOOTTTTTT!!'

Her eyes rolled towards me, and for one strange moment they looked like the eyes of someone else altogether – blood-shot and fierce and remote. But then Dr Hughes was ringing the bell for the nurses, and fixing a syringe of sedative, and I was ushered away from the bedside and into the corridor. I stood there, hearing her scream and fight inside, and I felt as helpless and isolated as I'd ever been in my whole life.


CHAPTER THREE

## THROUGH THE SHADOWS

A few minutes later, Dr Hughes came out of Karen Tandy's room, stripping off his gloves and his mask with weary resignation. I went up to him immediately.

'I'm sorry,' I told him. 'I just didn't realize it would have that effect.'

He rubbed his chin. 'It's not your fault. Neither did I. I've given her a light sedative and it should help her to calm down.'

We walked back to the changing-room together and took off our surgical robes.

'What worries me, Mr Erskine,' said Dr Hughes, 'is that she responded so *violently* to those words you came out with.

Up until then, she was okay – or at least as well as anybody could be expected to be with that kind of a tumour. But it seemed like you triggered something off there.'

'You're right,' I agreed. 'But exactly what was it? Why should a normal intelligent girl like Karen Tandy get so upset by the idea of an old Dutch galleon?'

Dr Hughes opened the door for me and led me out to the elevator.

'Don't ask me,' he said. 'You're supposed to be the mysticism specialist.'

He pressed the button for eighteen.

'What did the X-rays show you?' I asked. 'The ones you took in the operating theatre?'

'Nothing very clear,' answered Dr Hughes. 'When I said there seemed to be a foetus in that tumour, I should have said it was something foetus-*like*, but not exactly a baby in the accepted sense of the term. There is a growth of bone and flesh, which seems to have a systematic pattern of development, the same way that a baby has, but whether it's human or not, I can't say. I've called in a gynecological specialist, but he can't make it here until tomorrow.'

'But supposing tomorrow's too late? She looks – well, she looks as though she's going to *die*.'

Dr Hughes blinked in the bright light of the elevator. 'Yes, she does. I just wish to hell there was something I could do about it.'

The elevator reached the eighteenth floor and we stepped out. Dr Hughes led me into his office and went straight over to his filing cabinet and brought out a bottle of whisky. He sloshed out two large glassfuls, and we sat down and drank in silence.

After a while, he said: 'You know something, Mr Erskine. It's ridiculous and it's insane, but I believe that this nightmare has something to do with this tumour.'

'In what way?'

'Well, the two seem closely inter-related. I guess you spiritualists would think that the nightmare was causing the tumour, but I'd say it was the other way around – that the tumour is causing the nightmare. But whichever it is, it seems

52

to me that if we can discover more about the nightmare we can discover more about the condition.'

I swallowed a burning mouthful of neat Scotch.

'I've done all I can, Dr Hughes. I located the ship, and the ship seems to provoke a pretty severe reaction. But where can we go from here? I've told you – I'm only a quack when it comes to the real occult. I don't see what else I can do.'

Dr Hughes looked thoughtful. 'Supposing you do what I'm doing, Mr Erskine. Supposing you seek expert assistance.'

'What do you mean?'

'Well, surely all clairvoyants aren't – quacks, like you. Some of them must have genuine talent for investigating things like this.'

I put down my glass. 'Dr Hughes, you're really serious, aren't you? You really believe there's something occult going on here.

Dr Hughes shook his head. 'I didn't say that, Mr Erskine. All I'm doing is exploring every possibility. I learned a long time ago that, in medicine, it can be fatal to leave any avenue unexplored. You can't be narrow-minded, not when a human being's life is at risk.'

'So what do you suggest?' I asked him.

'Simply this, Mr Erskine. If you're interested in trying to save Karen Tandy from whatever it is that's making her ill, go out and find a real clairvoyant who can tell us just what this goddam ship thing is all about.

I thought for a while, and then I nodded. After all, I had nothing to lose. At least, I didn't *think* I had anything to lose. And who knows, I might end up with some real occult knowledge.

'Okay,' I said, swallowing the last of my whisky. 'I'm on my way.'

Back at my flat, I went straight into the kitchen and made myself four slices of cheese on toast. I hadn't eaten a thing all day, and I was feeling sick. I opened a can of Schiltz, and carried my meal into the sitting-room. I couldn't help sniffing around the place, just to see whether the evil spirit that had possessed Mrs Herz was still lurking in the shadows, but there was no evidence that anyone had been there. Mind you, I don't suppose that spirits leave footprints.

Munching my toast, I telephoned my friend Amelia Crusoe. Amelia ran a small knick-knackery store in the village, and I knew she was well into spiritualism and all that kind of stuff. She was a tall dark lady with long brown hair and soulful eyes, and she lived with a bearded guy called MacArthur, who made a living selling customized social security plates.

It was MacArthur who answered the phone. 'Who is this?' he said grumpily.

'Harry Erskine. I need to talk to Amelia. It's pretty urgent.'

'The Incredible Erskine!' said MacArthur. 'How's business in the up-and-up field of ripping off old ladies?'

'Pretty good,' I told him. 'How's the Engravaplate industry?'

'Not so bad,' he replied. 'It's not what you'd call a fulfilling career but it brings home the bacon. Hold on, Amelia's right here.'

Amelia sounded her usual soft, husky self.

'Harry? This *is* a surprise.'

'It's business, I'm afraid, Amelia. I was wondering if you could help me.'

'*Business?* Since when have you been into *business*?'

'Cut the sarcasm, Amelia, this is really important. I have a client who is very ill, I mean really, desperately ill. She's been having these terrible nightmares. I've talked to the doctors and they think it might be something to do with spiritualism.'

She whistled. 'The *doctors*? I didn't know doctors believed in spirits.'

'I don't think they do,' I told her. 'It's just that they're totally baffled, and they're willing to try anything to save her. Listen, Amelia, I need to get in touch with someone who really knows his stuff. I need a clairvoyant who's really together, and good. Do you know who could do that?'

'Harry, that's a pretty tall order. I mean, there are hundreds of clairvoyants, but most of them are about as good as you are. And, no offence meant, that means they're lousy.'

'No offence taken. I know my limitations.'

Amelia *ummed* and *ahhed* for a moment, and went through her address book, but after five minutes of searching she still hadn't come up with a name. In the end, she gave up.

'I just can't help you, Harry. Some of these guys are okay when it comes to fortune-telling, or putting you in touch with your long-lost Uncle Henry but I wouldn't trust any of them with anything serious.'

I bit my thumbnail. 'How about you?' I asked.

'Me? I'm not an expert. I know I'm a little bit *psychic*, but I'm not into all the greater arcana and that stuff.'

'Amelia,' I told her, 'you'll have to do. At least you're genuinely psychic, which is a damn sight more than I am. All you have to do is track down this *signal* or *nightmare* or whatever it is. Just give me a clue to where it could come from. I can do the rest by ordinary detective work.'

Amelia sighed. 'Harry, I'm *busy*. I'm going out to a dinner party this evening, and tomorrow I promised to take Janet's kids to the park, and on Monday I have to open the store, and I just don't have a single moment.'

'Amelia,' I said, 'a girl's life is at stake. That girl is up there in the Sisters of Jerusalem Hospital right at this very moment, and she's dying. Unless we can find out what her nightmares are all about, then she's just not going to last out.'

'Harry, I can't make myself responsible for every girl who's dying. This is a big city. Girls are always dying.'

I wrung the phone in my fist, as if I could squeeze Amelia into helping me. 'Amelia, *please*. Just tonight. Just for a couple of hours. That's all I'm asking.'

She put her hand over the phone and talked to Mac-Arthur. They burbled and murmured for a while, and then she came back on.

'Okay, Harry, I'll come. Where do you want me to be?'

I checked my watch. 'Come round to my place first. Then I think we'll have to go on to the girl's apartment. It seems

55

to be there that the dream started. Her aunt gets them as well, only not so bad. Amelia, I know this is a drag, but thank you.'

'I'll see you later,' she said, and put down the phone.

The next thing I did was dial Mrs Karmann, Karen Tandy's aunt. She was obviously sitting by the phone, waiting for news of Karen, because she answered almost immediately.

'Mrs Karmann? This is Harry Erskine.'

'Mr Erskine? I'm sorry, I thought it was the hospital.'

'Listen, Mrs Karmann, I went to visit Karen today. She's still pretty weak, but the doctors think her chances might be improved if they knew a little bit more about her.'

'I don't understand.'

'Well, you remember I called you yesterday about your dream. The one about the beach. Karen came and saw me and told me that she'd been having a dream just like yours. The doctors think it's possible that there might be something in the dream – some clue or other – that could help them to cure Karen's condition.'

'I still don't see what you're getting at, Mr Erskine. Why didn't Dr Hughes call me himself?'

'He didn't call you because he couldn't,' I explained. 'He's a medical specialist, and if any of his superiors found that he was messing around with spiritualism, they'd probably sack him on the spot. But he wants to try everything and anything to help Karen get well again. And that's why we need to know more about that dream you've both been having.'

Mrs Karmann sounded confused and anxious. 'But how can you do that? How can a *dream* give anyone a *tumour*?'

'Mrs Karmann, there are plenty of proven connections between people's minds and their state of health. I'm not saying that Karen's tumour is psychosomatic, but it's possible that her mental attitude toward it is making it more difficult for the doctors to cure her. They daren't operate until they understand what it is, and why it affects her so badly.'

'Well, Mr Erskine,' she said quietly, 'what do you want to do?'

'I've already contacted a friend of mine who's something of a medium,' I told her. 'What I'd like to do is hold a seance in your apartment, so that my friend can see if there are any vibrations around.'

'*Vibrations?* What kind of vibrations?'

'Anything, Mrs Karmann. Anything at all. We don't know what to expect until we find it.'

Mrs Karmann chewed this over for a few moments. Then she said: 'Well, Mr Erskine, I'm not at all sure. It somehow doesn't seem *right* to be doing something like that while Karen's so sick. I don't know what her parents would say if they found out.'

'Mrs Karmann,' I said. 'If Karen's parents knew you were trying everything within your power to help their daughter, then I don't see how they could possibly object. Please, Mrs Karmann. It's that important.'

'Well, all right, then, Mr Erskine. What time do you want to come round?'

'Give us an hour. Thank you, Mrs Karmann, you're terrific.'

Mrs Karmann sniffed. 'I know that already, Mr Erskine. I just hope you know what you're doing.' She wasn't the only one.

It was half-past ten by the time we had all gathered together at Mrs Karmann's apartment on East Eighty-Second. It was a big, warm place, decorated in a wealthy but anonymous style – big upholstered armchairs and settees, thick red velvet drapes, antique tables and paintings. It smelled of scent and old ladies.

Mrs Karmann herself was a fragile-looking woman with white bouffant hair, a pinched but once-pretty face, and a liking for floor-length silk dresses and lacy wraps. She gave me her soft and ring-laden hand to hold as I came in with Amelia and MacArthur, and I introduced everybody.

'I just pray that what we're doing won't make things *worse* for Karen,' she said.

MacArthur, with his big bearded face and his worn-out denims, went around the apartment bouncing on all the chairs to see how soft they were. Amelia, who was all dressed for dinner in a long red-printed kaftan, stayed quiet and withdrawn. She had thin, haunted-looking features, with big dark eyes and a pale full-lipped mouth that made her look as though she were going to start crying at any moment.

'Do you have a circular table, Mrs Karmann?' she asked softly.

'You can use the dining-table,' said Mrs Karmann. 'As long as you don't scratch it. It's a real genuine antique cherrywood.'

She led us through to the dining-room. The table was black and glossy, with a deep shine you could have drowned in. Above it was a glass teardrop chandelier. The walls of the room were decorated in dark green figured paper and there were gilded mirrors and oil paintings all around.

'This will do very well,' said Amelia. 'I think we ought to begin right away.'

The four of us sat down around the table and looked at each other rather selfconsciously. MacArthur was used to Amelia's spiritualism, but he was as sceptical as ever, and kept saying: 'Is there anyone there? Is there anyone there?'

'Quiet,' said Amelia. 'Harry, can you douse the lights please?'

I got up and switched off the lights, and the dining-room was plunged into total darkness. I groped my way back to my seat, and reached out blindly for the hands of Mrs Karmann and MacArthur. On my left, a hard male hand. On my right, a soft elderly female hand. The darkness was so complete that I felt as if a black blanket was being pressed against my face.

'Now concentrate,' said Amelia. 'Concentrate your minds on the spirits who occupy this room. Think of their souls, wandering through the ether. Think of their wants and their regrets. Try and imagine them as they float around us on their spiritual errands.'

'What the hell's a spiritual errand?' said MacArthur. 'You're telling me they have ghostly newspaper boys too?'

'Quiet,' said Amelia gently. 'This will be difficult, because we don't know who we're trying to contact. I'm trying to find a friendly spirit who will tell us what we need to know.'

We sat tight with our hands clasped while Amelia murmured a long incantation. I was trying desperately hard to think about the spirits who were moving through the room, but when you don't really believe in spirits, it's not exactly easy. I could hear Mrs Karmann breathing right next to me, and MacArthur's hand was fidgeting in mine. But at least he had the sense not to let go. From what I've heard, it's dangerous if you break the circle once the seance has begun.

'I am calling any spirit who can help me,' said Amelia. 'I am calling any spirit who can guide me.'

Gradually, I was able to concentrate more and more, directing my mind to the idea that there was really *something* or *somebody* around, some vibration in the room that would answer us. I felt the pulse of our whole circle go through my hands, I felt us join together in a complete circuit of minds and bodies. There seemed to be a current that flowed around and around the table, through our hands and our brains and our bodies, building up strength and voltage.

'Kalem estradim, ikona purista,' whispered Amelia. 'Venora, venora, optu luminari.'

The darkness stayed utterly dark, and there was nothing but the strange sensation that coursed through the four of us, the pulse that throbbed through our hands.

'Spirita halestim, venora suim,' breathed Amelia. 'Kalem estradim, ikon purista venora.'

I suddenly had the feeling that somebody had opened a window. There seemed to be a cold draught in the room, breezing around my ankles. It wasn't enough to make you feel uncomfortable, but there was a definite sensation of stirring air.

'Venora, venora, optu luminari,' chanted Amelia softly. 'Venora, venora, spirita halestim.'

The realization that I could *see* something in the darkness came so slowly and gradually that at first I thought it was just my eyes becoming accustomed to the gloom. The shadowy forms of Amelia and MacArthur and Mrs Karmann clotted into shape through the blackness, and I could see their eyes glittering. The table was like a bottomless pool between us.

Then I looked up and realized that the chandelier was glowing, with a dim and greenish light. The filaments of the bulbs seemed to crawl and flicker with current, like fireflies on a summer evening. But it was colder than summer, and the invisible draught made it colder and colder all the time.

'Are you there?' asked Amelia quietly. 'I can see your signs. Are you there?'

There was an odd rustling sound, as though there was someone else in the room, shifting and stirring. I could swear I heard *breathing* – deep, even breathing that wasn't the breathing of any of us.

'Are you there?' asked Amelia again. 'I can hear you now. Are you there?'

There was a long silence. The chandelier continued to glow dimly in the darkness, and I could hear the breathing more loudly now.

'*Talk*,' insisted Amelia. 'Tell us who you are. I command you to talk.'

The breathing seemed to change. It grew harsher and louder, and with each breath the chandelier pulsed and flickered. I could see its green reflections in the dark pool of the cherrywood table. Mrs Karmann's hand was digging deep into mine, but I hardly felt it. There was a persistent chilliness around the room, and the draught blew uncomfortably up my legs.

'Talk,' repeated Amelia. 'Speak and tell us who you are.'

'Christ,' said MacArthur impatiently, 'this is—'

'Ssshhh,' I told him. 'Just wait, MacArthur, it's coming.'

And it was coming. I stared at the centre of the table, and there seemed to be something shivering in the air a few inches above the surface. I felt the hairs on the back of my neck prickle and creep as the air twisted and flowed like smoke, then began to form itself into some sort of shape.

The breathing grew deep and loud and close, as though someone was actually breathing in my ear. The dim light of the chandelier faded altogether but the pouring snake of air in front of us had a luminescence all its own.

Underneath it, the actual wooden surface of the table began to *rise* in a lump. I bit my tongue until the sharp taste of blood flowed into my mouth. I was petrified with fear, but I couldn't turn away, couldn't refuse to look. The power of the circle held us all too strongly, and we could only sit there and stare at this terrifying spectacle in front of us.

The black shiny wood in the middle of the table formed into a *human face*, a man's face, with its eyes closed like a death mask.

'God,' said MacArthur, 'what is it?'

'Quiet,' whispered Amelia. I could see her white, intense expression by the unnatural light of the air. 'Leave this to me.'

Amelia leaned forward towards the frozen wooden face.

'Who are you?' she asked, almost cajolingly. 'What do you want with Karen Tandy?'

The face remained still. It was a fierce, deeply-lined face, the face of a powerful man in his late thirties, with a distinctively hooked nose, and wide full lips.

'What do you want?' asked Amelia again. 'What is it you're looking for?'

I could have been mistaken, but I thought I saw the black wooden lips move into a quiet and self-satisfied smile. The face stayed like that for a moment, and then melted away, and soon there was nothing there but the flat polished table.

The weird light faded, and we were back in darkness.

'Harry,' said Amelia. 'For God's sake put the lights on.'

I let go of MacArthur's hand, and Mrs Karmann's hand, and stood up. At that second, there was a shattering crack, and a brilliant white flash of light, and the windows smashed with a bomb-like explosion that sent glass spraying everywhere. The drapes flapped and billowed in the icy wind from the snowy night outside, and Mrs Karmann screamed in terror.

I went to the lights and snapped them on. Everything in the dining-room had been thrown around, as if a hurricane had come howling through. There were glasses and decanters on the floor, paintings were hanging askew, chairs were knocked over. The cherrywood dining table had split from one side to the other.

MacArthur stood up and came crunching across the carpet through the litter of glass. 'I've had enough, man. From now on, it's social security plates for me, and nothing else.'

'Harry,' called Amelia. 'Help me get Mrs Karmann through to the sitting room.'

Together we carried the old lady into the next room and laid her down on the settee. She was white and shivering, but she didn't seem to be hurt. I went over to the cocktail cabinet and poured her a large glass of brandy, and Amelia held it for her to sip.

'Is it all over?' she whimpered. 'What happened?'

'I'm afraid there's a bit of damage, Mrs Karmann,' I told her. 'The windows broke, and some of your glassware is smashed. I'm afraid the table's cracked too. But it's a clean split. Maybe you can get it repaired.'

'But what was it?' she said. 'That *face*!'

Amelia shook her head. MacArthur had found some cigarettes in a silver box, and he handed her one. She lit it with trembling hands, and blew the smoke out in a long unsteady stream.

'I don't know, Mrs Karmann. I'm not that expert as a medium. But whatever it was, it was very powerful. Usually, a spirit has to do what you tell it to do. This one was just showing us that it didn't give a damn what we thought of it.'

'But Amelia,' I said. 'Is that the thing that's been giving Karen Tandy all those nightmares?'

She nodded. 'I think so. I mean, it's so strong that it must be causing some kind of vibrations in this apartment. And I expect that's what Karen picked up in her dreams. When you're asleep, you're very receptive to vibrations, even weak ones, and these are much more powerful than any I've ever come across. There's something here that's possessed of real magical strength.'

I lit a cigarette myself and thought for a moment. 'Did you say *magical*?' I asked Amelia.

'Sure. Any spirit with that kind of control over itself

62

would have to be the spirit of somebody who knew about the occult when they were alive. It might even be a person who's still living today, and is able to float around as a spirit when they're asleep. It has been known.'

'Sounds like bullshit t'me,' said MacArthur. 'If I was Mrs Karmann, I'd take that table back and complain.'

I grinned. It was good to have a real sceptic around, even if he wasn't helping us much.

'Amelia,' I said. 'If you're saying that what we saw tonight was the spirit of someone magical, then there's an interesting tie-up. I was reading my Tarot cards the other evening, and I kept coming up with The Magician. No matter how I dealt or re-dealt them, I always ended up with the same card.'

Amelia brushed her long brown hair away from her eyes. 'In that case, I guess it's fair to suppose that whoever is doing this, whether they're alive or dead, is a magician. Or somebody like a magician.'

'Witch-doctor?' suggested MacArthur.

'Could be. I mean, he looked like some kind of African. Not just because the wood was black, but because of his lips, remember?'

Mrs Karmann sat up, clutching her glass of brandy. 'Well, I'll tell you what he reminded me of,' she said weakly. 'He reminded me of a cigar-store Indian.'

MacArthur snapped his fingers. 'That's it – Indian. The hooked nose, right, and the lips, and the high cheekbones. He's not a witch-doctor, he's a medicine man!'

Amelia brightened up. 'Listen,' she said. 'I have quite a few books on Indians. Why don't we go back to my place and see what we can find out about medicine men? Mrs Karmann, do you think you'll be all right now?'

'Oh, you go ahead,' said the old lady. 'I'll stay across the hall with my neighbour Mrs Routledge – and Karen's parents will be here later. If you think that any of this can help poor Karen, then the sooner you get going the better.'

'Mrs Karmann,' said Amelia, 'you're an angel.'

'Not yet awhile, I hope,' smiled Mrs Karmann. 'Not yet awhile.'

Back in the untidy jumble of Amelia's apartment in the Village, surrounded by books and magazines and tapestries and pictures and old hats and half a bicycle, we went through a dozen volumes on Indian lore. Surprisingly, there wasn't much about medicine men, apart from stuff on buffalo magic and rain dances and battle spells. Out of eleven books, nothing gave us any clues about the wooden death-mask on Mrs Karmann's table.

'Maybe we're totally mistaken,' said Amelia. 'Perhaps the spirit is somebody living today. I mean, a hooked nose doesn't have to be Indian. It could be Jewish.'

'Wait a minute,' I told her. 'Have you any other history books, or anything at all that might contain a cross-reference to Indians or medicine-men?'

Amelia scuffled through a couple of heaps of books, and came up with a history of early settlements in the United States, and the first volume of a three-volume study of New York. I went to the indexes and looked up Indians.

The book on early settlements contained nothing more than the usual generalizations about Indian civilization. In those early days people were more in the mood for land-grabbing than studying the indigenous culture of the natives. But the book on New York had an illustration which gave me the biggest break I'd had since I'd found Karen Tandy's nightmare ship in the library.

I'd seen the drawing before – in school-books and history books – but it was only when I came across it that night in Amelia Crusoe's apartment that I realized just what its implications were. It was a sketch engraving of the tip of an island. On the shore was a small cluster of houses, a windmill, and a high-walled fort in the shape of a cross of Lorraine. There were ships standing offshore, and canoes and jolly-boats paddling around in the foreground.

The largest of the ships was identical to Karen Tandy's nightmare vessel and the picture's caption bore the connection out. It read: 'Earliest known view of New Amsterdam, 1651. The director-general of the Dutch West India Company lived in this small but important settlement.'

I passed the book over to Amelia. 'Look at this,' I said. 'This is the exact ship that Karen Tandy dreamed about – and look, there are half-a-dozen Indians in that canoe. This is what New York was like, three hundred and twenty years ago.'

She studied the picture carefully. 'Harry,' she said, 'this could be it. This could be just what we're looking for. Supposing there was an Indian medicine man in New York, or New Amsterdam, all those centuries ago, and supposing that Karen actually picked up his vibrations in the same place that he once used to live.'

'That's right,' put in MacArthur, scratching his beard. 'There musta been an Indian village on East Eighty-Second Street. Mind you, it sometimes looks as though there still is.'

I sat up and stretched my aching back. 'That whole business about "de boot" would fit in then. If this guy was a medicine man at the time the Dutch settled on Manhattan, then the only words of European he'd be likely to know would be *Dutch*. "De boot, mijnheer," would be his way of saying something about the ship. And judging from Karen's dream, he was afraid of the ship. She told me it seemed to her like an alien ship – almost like something from Mars. And I guess that's just how it *would* appear to an Indian.'

Amelia found a cigarette in a crumpled pack and lit it. 'But why is he so *malignant*?' she asked. 'And how does that tie in with Karen's tumour? I mean, what's the tumour all about?'

Unexpectedly, MacArthur said: 'I've found it.' He'd been looking through a large dusty encyclopedia, and he marked the page and passed it over to me.

'Medicine Men,' I read aloud, 'were often powerful magicians who were said to be capable of extraordinary supernatural acts. They were believed to be immortal, and if threatened, could destroy themselves by drinking blazing oil, and be reborn at any time or place in the future or past by impregnating themselves into the body of a man, woman or animal.'

Amelia's eyes were wide. 'Is that all it says?' she asked me.

65

'That's all,' I told her. 'After that, it goes on to rain dances again.'

'Then that means that Karen is—'

'Pregnant,' I said, shutting the book. 'In a manner of speaking, she's about to give birth to a primitive savage.'

'But Harry,' said Amelia, 'what the hell can we do?'

MacArthur stood up and went in search of some beer in the icebox. 'All you can do,' he said, 'is wait until the medicine man hatches, then give him a doze of blazing oil. That should get rid of him for you.'

'That's impossible,' I told him. 'By the time that medicine man is ready to be born, Karen Tandy will be dead.'

'I know,' said MacArthur glumly, sipping beer. 'But I don't see what the hell else you could do.'

I went across to the phone. 'Well, the first thing I'm going to do is call the hospital. Maybe Dr Hughes will have some ideas. At least we have a theory about it now, which is a damn sight more than we had a couple of hours ago.'

I dialled the Sisters of Jerusalem Hospital, and asked for Dr Hughes. When he answered, he sounded even more tired than ever. It was nearly one o'clock in the morning, and he must have been on duty all day.

'Dr Hughes? This is Harry Erskine.'

'What do you want, Mr Erskine? Have you got some news of your ghost?'

'I found a medium, Dr Hughes, and we held a seance tonight in Karen's apartment. There was some kind of manifestation – a face. All of us saw it. We've been checking through books on Indian history and stuff like that, and we think it might be an Indian medicine man of the seventeenth century. According to one of these books – hold on – Indian medicine men "if threatened, could destroy themselves by drinking blazing oil, and be reborn at any time or place in the future or past by impregnating themselves into the body of a man, woman or animal". Do you think that fits, Dr Hughes?'

There was a long silence on the other end of the telephone.

Then Dr Hughes said: 'Mr Erskine, I don't know what to

almost fits too well. But if it is true, what can
say . . . do to destroy such a creature? Dr Snaith made more
anyone . . . afternoon, and it's absolutely clear that if we do
tests th . . . to remove or kill that foetus, then Karen Tandy
anyth . . . The thing has become an integral part of her own
wil . . . ystem.'

. . . she, doctor? Is she conscious?'

. . . bout, but she's not responding too well. If this
. . . es on growing at the same rate, I can only say that
. . . dead within two or three days. Dr Snaith thinks
. . . ly.'

. . . ow about the gynecological expert?'

He's as baffled as the rest of us,' said Dr Hughes. 'He
confirmed that the foetus wasn't a normal child, but he
agreed with me that it has all the characteristics of a fast-
growing parasitic organism. If you believe it's a medicine
man, Mr Erskine, then your opinion is just as valid as any of
the opinions we've come up with here.'

Amelia came and stood beside me and raised her eyebrows
questioningly.

'How is she?' she asked.

I put my hand over the phone. 'Bad. The doctors don't
think she'll last until Tuesday.'

'But what about the thing – the medicine man?' asked
Amelia. 'Does he think *that* will grow and survive? I mean,
Jesus—'

I spoke to Dr Hughes again. 'Dr Hughes, my friend here
asks what's going to happen to the foetus. Supposing it's still
alive when Karen Tandy dies? What are you going to do
about it?'

Dr Hughes didn't hesistate. 'Mr Erskine, in that event we
will do what we always do. If it is a child, and it's normal
and healthy, we'll do everything we can to save it. If it turns
out to be a monster – well, we have injections that can dis-
pose of it quietly and quickly.'

'And if it's a medicine man?' I asked warily.

He paused. 'Well, if it's a medicine man – I don't know.
But I can't see how it *could* be, Mr Erskine. I'm willing to go
some way towards the occult but how on earth could she

give birth to a three hundred year old Indian? I me[an, come] on, let's be serious.'

'Dr Hughes, it was you who suggested we try and [come out] if there was anything occult going on here. And you[d out] that my opinion was as valid as anyone else's.'

Dr Hughes sighed. 'I know that, Mr Erskine. I'm [v] But you have to admit it sounds pretty crazy.'

'Crazy or not, I think we ought to try and do someth[ing] about it.'

'What do you suggest?' said Dr Hughes dully.

'Something you recommended has worked once, D[r] Hughes. You said I ought to bring an expert in, and I did. I think it's time we went looking for another expert – somebody who knows more than we do about Indian lore and mysticism. Give me some time and I'll try to dig somebody up. There's bound to be someone at Harvard or Yale who knows.'

'Could be,' said Dr Hughes. 'Okay, Mr Erskine. Thanks for your interest and your help. Don't hesitate to call me if there's anything else you want to know.'

I put the phone down slowly. Amelia and MacArthur stood beside me, just as weary as I was, but eager to help now, and really interested. They'd seen the face on the cherrywood table, and they *believed*. Whatever the spirit was, whether it was an Indian medicine man or a malignant ghost of the present, they wanted to help me fight it.

'If you ask me,' said MacArthur, 'the Dutch should have kept their twenty-four dollars and left Manhattan to the Indians. It looks as though the original owners are getting their revenge.'

I sat down and rubbed my eyes. 'It looks that way, MacArthur. Now let's get some sleep. We've got a lot to do tomorrow.'

CHAPTER FOUR

# ACROSS THE TWILIGHT

It took us four hours to track down Dr Ernest Snow. A friend of Amelia's knew someone at Harvard who knew someone else who was a student of anthropology, and in turn the student of anthropology put us on to Dr Snow.

His credentials were impressive. He had written five monographs on Indian religious and magical rites, and a book called *Rituals and Lore of the Hidatsa*. What's more, he lived within reach, in Albany, New York.

'Well,' said MacArthur, yawning through the gloom of a dark and wintry Sunday morning, 'are you going to phone him?'

'I guess so,' I told him. 'I was just wondering whether we haven't gone off on the wrong track.'

'What do you mean?' asked Amelia.

'Well, I mean this whole Indian business. We don't really have any evidence to support it. Just because the face on the table looked something like a Red Indian, there's no real reason to think that he really was.'

Amelia shrugged. 'But what else have we got to go on? And there is all this stuff about rebirth. Come on, Harry, we have to try it.'

'Okay, then, here goes,' I said, and picked up the phone. I dialled Dr Snow's number and listened to it ringing. He seemed to take a long time to answer.

'Snow here,' said a clipped, crisp voice.

'Dr Snow, I'm sorry to disturb you on Sunday, but when I tell you why I'm calling, I hope you'll understand. My name's Harry Erskine, and I'm a professional clairvoyant.'

'You're a *what*?' snapped Dr Snow. He didn't sound very amused.

'I tell fortunes. I work in New York City.'

There was a tense pause, and then Dr Snow said: 'Mr Erskine, it's very good of you to call me on a Sunday morning and tell me that. But I don't understand why your being a fortune-teller is so particularly urgent.'

'It's like this, Dr Snow. I have a client who's in hospital right now, a young girl, and she's very sick. She has a kind of tumour on her neck, and the doctors are pretty baffled.'

'I'm sorry to hear that,' said Dr Snow, 'but I don't quite see what it's got to do with me. I'm a doctor of anthropology, not of medicine.'

'That's exactly why I'm calling you, Dr Snow. You see, I believe my client is being used as a host for the reincarnation of an Indian medicine man. I think that tumour of hers is actually the foetus of a redskin. You've heard of that, haven't you? The way they drank blazing oil and got themselves reborn in the past or the future.'

This time, there was a longer and tenser pause. Then Dr Snow said: 'Are you serious, Mr . . .'

'Erskine.'

'Mr Erskine, do you know what you're saying? You're telling me that there is somebody in New York City *today*, alive now, who is harbouring a reincarnated medicine man?'

'That's exactly it, sir.'

'Is this some kind of a hoax? Are you putting me on? Students do that, you know.'

'I realize that, sir. But if you give me the chance to come and talk to you for half-an-hour, I think you'll realize that we're not kidding. If you want to check up on me, you can ring Dr Hughes at the Sisters of Jerusalem Hospital. We're doing this work with his approval.'

'We?'

'Myself and two friends. One of them is a medium.'

I could almost hear Dr Snow's mind churning around on the end of the telephone. Amelia and MacArthur stared at me nervously as I waited for the old man's reply.

'All right,' he said finally. 'I suppose you want to come and see me today?'

'As soon as possible, Dr Snow. I know this is a real inconvenience, but a girl is dying.'

'Oh, it's no inconvenience. My wife's sister is coming over today, and the less I have to see of her, the better I like it. Come up anytime.'

'Thank you, Dr Snow.'

I put the phone down. It was as simple as that. I'm always amazed how readily and quickly people will accept the occult and the supernatural, once the evidence is there in front of their eyes. Dr Snow had probably read about medicine man reincarnation for years, without really believing it was possible, but as soon as someone had told him it had actually happened, he was ready to accept it without a qualm.

Anyway, I grabbed my car keys and put on my herringbone coat.

'Who's coming to Albany?' I asked, and Amelia and MacArthur both got up to get ready.

'I hate to say this,' said MacArthur, 'but this is a damn sight more interesting than selling social security plates.'

Dr Snow lived in a small, tight, brick-built house on the outskirts of Albany. It was surrounded by dark, mournful cypress trees, and its windows were hung with yellowed lace. The sky was threatening and metallic as we drove up through the thick slush and ice, and there was a keen persistent wind blowing from the north-east. There was a strange silence around, like the silence of children waiting for a teacher they feared.

We stood around on the doorstep clapping our hands to get the circulation back, and I rang the bell. It went ding-donggg, deep in the recesses of the old house.

The door opened, and Dr Snow stood there. He was a tall, bent man with white monkish hair and gold-rimmed spectacles. He was wearing a maroon cardigan with baggy pockets, and plaid carpet slippers.

'Mr Erskine?' he said. 'You'd better come in.'

We shuffled into the gloomy hallway. There was a strong smell of lavender polish, and a long-case clock ticked wearily in the corner. We took off our coats, and Dr Snow led us through into a chilly parlour. There were fierce Indian

71

masks all around the walls, contrasting with the English delicacy of stuffed linnets in glass domes, and faded little Stevengraphs.

'Sit down,' said Dr Snow. 'You'd better explain what this is all about. My wife will bring you some coffee in a moment. I'm afraid we don't drink liquor in this house.'

MacArthur looked decidedly glum at that. There was a flask of bourbon in the car, but he was too polite to ask if he could go and get it.

Dr Snow sat down on a hard little cane chair, and crossed his hands in front of him. Amelia and I shared a low and uncomfortable settee, and MacArthur perched himself on the window seat, so that he could stare out at the snowy trees.

As briefly as I could, I explained Karen Tandy's condition to Dr Snow, and told him about the seance we had held the night before. He listened quite intently, occasionally asking me questions about Karen and her aunt, and about the apparition we had seen on Mrs Karmann's cherrywood table.

When I'd finished, he sat there for a while with his hands clasped, and considered. Then he said: 'From what you've told me, Mr Erskine, the case of this unfortunate girl sounds genuine. I think you're right. There is only one other recorded case of a person being chosen as the host for a medicine man's rebirth, and that was in 1851, at Fort Berthold, on the Upper Missouri, among the Hidatsa Indians. A young Indian girl had a swelling on her arm, which eventually grew so large that it overwhelmed her, and she died. Out of the swelling emerged a complete and fully-grown man, who was said to be a magician of the tribe from fifty years previous.

'There was very little documentary evidence to support the truth of this story, and up until now it has been regarded as myth or legend. I have even called it that myself in my book on the Hidatsas. But the parallels with your Miss Tandy seem so close that I can't see what else it could be. There are also stories among the Kiowas that medicine men could appear as trees, and talk to people of the tribe. Apparently trees and wood have a mystic life-force of their own which medicine men were able to exploit for their own purpose. And that is why I believe your story of the cherrywood table. I thought at first you were trying to hoax me, but your evidence is overwhelmingly convincing.'

'So you believe it?' asked Amelia, brushing her hair away from her eyes.

'Yes,' said Dr Snow, peering back at her through his spectacles. 'I do believe it. I also took the trouble to do what you suggested, and I called Dr Hughes at the Sisters of Jerusalem. He confirmed what you told me. He also told me that Miss Tandy was in a critical condition, and that anything that anyone could do to save her would be very important.'

'Dr Snow,' I said, 'is there any way to fight this medicine man? Is there anything we can do to destroy him, before he kills Karen Tandy?'

Dr Snow frowned. 'What you have to understand, Mr Erskine, is that the magic of the Indians was very powerful and far-ranging. They drew no clear distinction between the natural and the supernatural, and every Indian saw himself as being in close touch with the spirits that ruled his existence. The plains Indians, for instance, spent as much time on their religious ceremonies and medicine signs as they did on perfecting their hunting skills. They considered it important to be able to hunt their buffalo with craftsmanship and cunning, but at the same time they thought that only the spirits would give them the strength and the bravery to be able to carry out the hunt successfully.

'The Indians were seekers of visions and practicians of ritual, devoted to ceremonies that brought them into close touch with the cosmos. They were in fact one of the great magical societies of modern times. Much of their sevret lore has been lost to us, but there is no doubt at all that they had real and extraordinary powers.'

Amelia looked up. 'What you're trying to tell us, Dr Snow, is that none of us have enough magical power to be able to combat this medicine man . . .'

The doctor nodded. 'I'm afraid you're right. And if the medicine man is really three hundred years old, he comes from a time when the magic of the Indians was still amazingly strong. It would have been pure ethnic occult art, undiluted with European preconceptions, and unimpressed by Christianity.

'The occult spirits of North America, at the time of the early settlers, were a million times more powerful and dangerous than any of the devils or demons of Europe. You see, a spirit can only work its magic in the world of humans through the medium of men and women who believe in it and understand it. Spirits do have an independent existence, but they can have no material power in our own material world unless they are summoned, consciously or subconsciously. And if no one believes in a particular spirit, or is able to understand it, it cannot be summoned, and so it remains in limbo.

'The demons of Europe were pitiful compared with the demons of the Red Indians. All they were – or *are*, if you still believe in them – was *opposites* to the good and holy tenets of Christianity. In *The Exorcist*, the story uses the demon Pazuzu, the personification of sickness and ill health. To the red man, a demon like that would have been ridiculous – nothing more terrifying than a mongrel dog. The whole concept of life and health and the meaning of physical existence was rolled up in the red man's equivalent spirit, and that made this particular spirit an incredible being with monstrous powers.

'To my mind, the real decline of the red man came not so much through the treachery and greed of the whites, but through the erosion of the occult powers of the medicine men. When the red tribes saw the scientific marvels of the white man, they were unduly impressed, and lost faith in their own magic. It's arguable that this magic, if it had been used properly, could have saved them.'

Amelia interrupted the doctor with a question. 'But what about Karen Tandy's medicine man? What do you suppose he was doing? I mean, why would he want to be reborn in her?'

Dr Snow scratched his ear. 'It's difficult to say. From what you've told me about her dream of the Dutch ship, I'd hazard a guess that the medicine man's existence was being threatened by the Dutch settlement on Manhattan. Maybe the medicine man had tried to prevent the rest of his tribe from selling the island so cheaply. With the kind of occult powers that medicine men possessed, he may have been able to see how instrumental the possession of Manhattan by white men would be in the development of a white America. It's also possible that the Dutch, being strict Calvinists, considered the medicine man an evil influence, and were out to destroy him. Whatever happened, he obviously thought that the only way he could escape was by leaving his seventeenth-century existence, and reappearing in some other time. I wouldn't have thought he chose Karen Tandy deliberately. She probably just happened to be a receptive home for his reincarnation, at the right place at the right time.'

'Dr Snow,' I asked him. 'If we're not equipped to fight with this medicine man, then do you have any idea who might be? I mean, can anyone at all summon enough power to destroy him for good?'

Dr Snow looked thoughtful. 'This is such a remarkable occurrence that one wishes that a young girl's life wasn't involved. Just think of it, Mr Erskine, within two or three days we could actually meet an Indian medicine man, living and breathing, from another time far in America's past. It seems almost criminal to think of destroying him.'

MacArthur turned round from his seat by the window. 'We all know the wonders of anthropology, Dr Snow, but this is a human life we're trying to save here. Karen Tandy didn't *ask* to have this witch doctor grow inside her. I think it's up to us to do everything we can to save her.'

'Yes, I know,' said Dr Snow. 'But there really is only one way we can do that.'

'And what's that?' Amelia asked. 'Is it difficult?'

'It could be. And dangerous. You see, the only person who can fight a medicine man is another medicine man. There are one or two around still, in some of the reservations. But none of them would be nearly as powerful as this man. They might know some of the old rituals, but it's doubtful if they'd have anything like the same abilities and strength. And if they couldn't beat him, if they couldn't destroy him utterly, they'd inevitably be killed themselves.'

'But wait a minute,' I said. 'That medicine man is still in the process of rebirth. He hasn't grown to his full size, and he's obviously not as strong as he could be when he's completely redeveloped. If we could get hold of another medicine man now, we could kill him before he emerges.'

'It would be very dangerous,' said Dr Snow. 'Not only to our own medicine man, but to the girl as well. They might both die.'

'Doctor,' I said. 'She's going to die anyway.'

'Well, I guess that's true. But how are we going to persuade some poor old peaceful reservation Indian to risk his life for a white girl he doesn't even know?'

'We bribe him,' said MacArthur.

'What with?' asked Amelia.

'Maybe we ought to talk to Karen Tandy's parents,' I suggested. 'They'll be in town by now. They're obviously quite wealthy, and I guess a couple of thousand dollars would take care of it. Dr Snow, do you think you could *find* a medicine man?'

Dr Snow rubbed his chin. 'Oh, that shouldn't be too difficult. I have a friend in South Dakota who could probably dig someone up. We'd have to pay to fly the medicine man to New York, naturally, even supposing that he'd agree to do it.'

'I think it's time we talked to Karen Tandy's parents,' I said. 'They have a right to know what's going on, and we're obviously going to need some cash. Dr Snow, can I ask a favour of you?'

'Certainly,' said Dr Snow. 'This case is fascinating, and I'd feel privileged to help.'

'Could you call your friend in South Dakota and ask him to start looking for the most powerful medicine man he can find? Then if Karen Tandy's parents do agree to bring someone in, at least we'll be ready. Could you do that?'

'With pleasure,' said Dr Snow.

We left the Snows' house around five o'clock. It was already night, and the wind hit us in the face like a bucketful of razor blades. We drove off into the weird half-light of icebound landscape, tired and chilly, but even more determined to save Karen Tandy from the mysterious enemy which had invaded her body. The first thing I wanted to do when I got back to New York was to check up on how she was, and ask Dr Hughes just how much time he thought we had left. There was no point in going to all the expense of bringing an Indian medicine man from South Dakota if Karen was already dead, or just about to die.

'You know something,' said MacArthur, resting his legs across the Cougar's back seat, 'I think there's something like historic justice in all this. I mean, I feel sorry for Karen, but as you sow you certainly shall reap, don't you think?'

Amelia turned round and smirked at him. 'MacArthur,' she said, 'I love your beard and I love your body, but your philosophy stinks.'

I dropped Amelia and MacArthur in the Village, and then I drove up to the Sisters of Jerusalem to check on Karen. I was pretty exhausted by the time I got there, and I went into the men's room to wash up and tidy my hair. When I looked at myself in the glass, I looked pale and tired and frail, and I began to wonder how the hell I would summon up the strength to battle with a medicine man from the golden age of Indian magic.

I found Dr Hughes in his office, reading a pile of reports by the light of his desk lamp.

'Mr Erskine,' he said, 'you're back. How did it go?'

I flopped down in the chair opposite him. 'I think we know what's going on, anyway. But whether we'll be able to fight it or not – well, that's another question.'

He listened seriously while I explained what Dr Snow had said. I also told him that we were trying to find a rival medicine man to fly into New York.

Dr Hughes got up from his chair and went over to the window. He stared down at the crawling lights of traffic, and the first spinning flakes of a fresh snowfall.

'I just hope to God that none of this leaks out to the newspapers,' he said. 'It's difficult enough keeping it quiet from the rest of the specialists and surgeons involved. But just think about it — the world's second or third leading specialist on tumours has to bring in a redskin from the plains of South Dakota, some mumbo-jumbo artist with warpaint and bones, because he can't manage to deal with a tumour by himself.'

'You know as well as I do that this isn't any ordinary tumour,' I said. 'And you can't fight a magic tumour with ordinary methods. The proof of what you're doing will be in the cure.'

Dr Hughes looked away from the window. 'And supposing she doesn't get cured? What do I say then? I brought in a redskin medicine man, but that wasn't any use, either?'

'Dr Hughes—'

'It's okay, Mr Erskine. I don't really have any qualms about this. I've seen enough tumours in my life to know that this isn't anything like an ordinary condition. And I believe your theory, about the Indans. I don't know why I believe it, but I can't see any other rational explanation. None of my colleagues has even got as much as a wild guess.'

'How is she, doctor?' I asked him. 'Is the tumour still growing?'

'Do you want to see for yourself?' he said. 'It's got worse since you last saw her, yesterday.'

'If it's okay. I'll try not to upset her, like last time.'

In silence, we took the elevator to the tenth floor. In silence, we put on masks and robes. In silence, we walked down the corridor to Karen Tandy's room, and opened the door.

It was grotesque. Karen Tandy was lying on her front now, her face as white as the sheet it was resting on. The tumour lay bloatedly on her back, a fat white bladder of swollen skin. It was as big as a pillow, and it seemed to shift and bulge and ease itself from time to time, a great pulpy growth with a malignant life of its own.

'God,' I said softly. 'It's grown enormous.'

'And it's getting bigger all the time,' said Dr Hughes. 'Come here, feel it.'

I stepped cautiously up to the bedside. The tumour was so big that it was hard to believe it was actually part of the girl, who lay under it, carrying it on her back like a sickening hunch. I gingerly reached out with my finger tips and pressed it. It seemed firm and distended, but there was a sensation of something slithery inside. In fact, it felt exactly like the stomach of a pregnant woman.

'Can't you just kill it?' I asked Dr Hughes. 'It must be the size of a small child by now. Can't you just stick a scalpel into it?'

Dr Hughes shook his head. 'I wish I could. I'd like to chop it off with a meat cleaver, if you want to know the truth. But every X-ray shows that the nervous system of this creature is inextricably bound up with Karen's nervous system. Any surgical attempt to remove it would kill her at once. They're not so much like mother and child — they're more like Siamese twins.'

'Can she talk at all?'

'She hasn't said anything for several hours. We took her out of bed to weigh her this morning, and she spoke a couple of words then, but nothing that any of us could understand.'

'You weighed her? Is she in a bad way?'

Dr Hughes tucked his hands in the pockets of his robe and looked sadly down at his dying patient. 'She hasn't lost any weight at all — but she hasn't gained any either. Whatever this tumour is, it's taking all its sustenance directly from her. Every ounce it grows, it takes from Karen.'

'Have her parents been in touch?'

'They came in this morning. The mother was very upset. I told them that we were going to try for an operation, but naturally I didn't say anything about the medicine man stuff. They were angry enough at me as it was, because I hadn't been able to operate already. If I'd started telling them about oldtime red Indians, they would have thought I was off my head.'

I took one last look at Karen Tandy, lying white and silent under her sickening burden, and then we left the room and went back to Dr Hughes' office on the eighteenth floor.

'Do you think her parents will be hard to convince?' I asked him. 'The problem is that all this is going to take money. We're going to have to bribe the medicine man, and

79

we're going to have to pay for his plane fare and his hotel, not to mention what the hell might happen if he gets hurt in the battle. I'd love to help, but us clairvoyants are not exactly Rockefellers. I doubt if I could raise more than three or four hundred bucks.'

Dr Hughes looked glum. 'I could get the money out of the hospital under normal circumstances, but I don't see how I can possibly indent for the use of a *medicine man*. No, I think her parents have a right to know what's going on, anyway, and make the choice for themselves. After all, the life of their daughter is at stake.'

'Do you want me to talk to them?' I asked him.

'You could do, if you want to. They're staying at Karen's aunt's place, on eighty-second. If you get into any trouble, ask them to call me and confirm that you have my support.'

'Okay,' I said. 'Now, how about a drink?'

'Good thinking,' said Dr Hughes, and fetched out his bottle of bourbon. He poured out a couple of large ones, and I swallowed mine just as it came, fiery and revitalizing after a weary day's driving to Albany and back. I sat back and Dr Hughes offered me a cigarette.

We smoked for a while in silence, then I said: 'Dr Hughes—'

'Why don't you call me Jack? This hospital's pretty formal. It gives the patients confidence if they hear people being called "doctor" all the time. But I don't think that's the kind of confidence you need.'

'Okay, Jack. I'm Harry.'

'That's better. Nice to know you, Harry.'

I swallowed some more bourbon. 'Jack,' I said, 'have you stopped to consider exactly what we're doing here and why we're doing it? I don't know Karen Tandy much better than I know you. I just sometimes think, what the hell am I doing driving to Albany and back for someone I don't even know.'

Jack Hughes grinned. 'Don't you think that's a question that everybody who helps other people asks themselves? I ask myself that question ten times a day. When you're a doctor of medicine, you're taken for granted. People come to you when they're sick, and think you're terrific, but as soon as they're well again, you cease to be interesting. Some patients are grateful. I get Christmas cards every year from some of them. But most of them wouldn't even recognize me if I bumped into them on the street.'

'I guess you're right,' I said.

'I know I'm right,' replied Jack. 'But I think this case is something different. I'm not interested in this case for the usual reasons. The way I see it, this thing that's growing in Karen Tandy represents a whole medical and cultural problem.'

'What do you mean?'

Jack Hughes stood up and came over to sit on the edge of his desk right next to me.

'Look at it this way,' he said. 'The fascinating thing about America is that it was always supposed to be a brand-new nation, free of oppression and free of guilt. But from the moment the white man settled here, there was a built-in time-bomb of guilt. In the Declaration of Independence, there is even an attempt to gloss over this guilt, you remember? Jefferson wrote about "the merciless Indian Savages, whose known rule of warfare is an undistinguished destruction of all ages, sexes and conditions". Right from the beginning, the Indian has not counted as an individual who is endowed by his Creator with those certain inalienable rights.

'Gradually, the guilt of what we did to the Indians has eroded our sense of owning and belonging to our own country. This isn't *our* land, Harry. This is the land we *stole*. We make jokes about Peter Minuit buying Manhattan Island for twenty-four dollars. But, these days, that kind of deal would be considered a theft, an out-and-out con. Then there's all this business about Wounded Knee, and every other Indian massacre. We're guilty, Harry. There's nothing we could or should do about the past, but we're still guilty.'

I had never heard Jack Hughes speaking so eloquently. I watched him drag at his cigarette and brush some ash from his crumpled pants.

'That's why this case is so interesting – and so frightening,' he said. 'If it's really true, this whole medicine man bit, then for the first time ever, white men with a fully-developed sense of guilt are going to come into contact with a red man from the earliest days of our settlement. Today, we think about Indians in a totally different way. Back in the seventeenth century, they were savages and they were standing in the way of our need for land and our greed for material wealth. These days, now we have everything we want, we can afford to be softer and more tolerant. I know we've all been talking about destroying this medicine man, and fighting him, but don't you feel some sympathy for him as well?'

I stubbed out my cigarette. 'I feel some sympathy for Karen Tandy.'

'Yes,' said Jack, 'of course you do. She's our patient, and her life is in terrible danger. We can't forget that. But don't you feel *anything* for this savage from the past?'

In a strange way, Jack Hughes was right. I did feel something. There was a tiny part of my brain that wanted him to survive. If there was a way in which both Karen Tandy and the medicine man could live, then that would be the way I would choose. I was frightened of him, I was terrified of his powers and his mastery of the occult, but at the same time he was like a mythical hero of legend, and to destroy him would mean destroying something of America's heritage. He was a lone survivor from our country's shameful past, and to kill him would be like grinding out the last spark of the spirit that had given the United States such a colourful and mystical background. He was the last representative of original American magic.

Just then, the telephone bleeped. Jack Hughes picked it up, and said: 'Hughes.'

Someone was speaking very excitedly on the other end. Jack Hughes frowned and nodded, and said: 'When? Are you sure? Well, have you tried forcing it? What do you mean, you can't?

Finally, he laid the receiver down.

'Is anything wrong?' I asked.

'I don't know. It's Karen. McEvoy says they can't get the door open. There's something going on in her room, and they can't get the door open.'

82

We left the office and rushed down the corridor to the elevator. There were two nurses in there with a trolleyful of bottles and kidney bowls and we wasted precious seconds while they manoeuvred it out of the way. We got in, pressed the button for ten, and sank downwards.

'What the hell do you think has happened?' I asked Jack tersely.

He shook his head. 'Who knows?'

'I just hope to God that medicine man isn't able to use his powers already,' I said. 'If he can, we're totally sunk.'

'I don't know,' replied Jack Hughes. 'Come on, we're here.'

The elevator doors hissed open, and we ran swiftly down the corridor to Karen Tandy's room. Dr McEvoy was standing outside with two male nurses and Selena, the radiologist.

'What's happened?' snapped Jack.

'She was left alone for less than a couple of seconds,' explained Dr McEvoy. 'The nurses were changing over their duty. When Michael here tried to get back in, he couldn't open the door. And look.'

We peered into Karen Tandy's room through the glass panel in the door. I was shocked to see that she was no longer lying in bed. The sheets and blankets were rumpled and pushed aside.

'There,' whispered Jack. 'In the corner.'

I angled my head and saw Karen Tandy standing at the far corner of the room. Her face was horribly white, and her lips were drawn back over her teeth in a stretched and grotesque grin. She was leaning forward under the weight of the huge distended bulge on her back, and her long white hospital nightgown was torn from her shoulders, revealing her shrunken breasts and prominent ribs.

'Good God,' said Jack, 'she's *dancing*.'

He was right. She was hopping slowly from foot to foot, in the same slow silent waltz that Mrs Herz had been dancing. It seemed as if she were skipping to a soundless drum, a noiseless flute.

'We have to break in there,' ordered Jack. 'She could kill herself, running about like that.'

'Michael, Wolf,' said Dr McEvoy to the two male nurses. 'Do you think you can get your shoulders to the door?'

'We'll try, sir,' said Wolf, a burly young German with a dark crew-cut. 'I'm sorry about this, sir, I didn't realize.'

'Just get the door down,' said Jack.

The two nurses stood back a yard or two, and then rushed at the door together. It splintered and cracked, and the glass broke. A strange cold draught, like the draught that had blown during our seance in Mrs Karmann's apartment, flowed icily from the jagged hole.

'Again,' said Jack.

Michael and Wolf stepped back again, and smashed against the door once again. This time, they wrenched it right off its hinges, and it twisted open. Dr Hughes stepped in and went straight up to Karen, where she was bobbing and hopping on the rug. The great swollen hunch on her back was wobbling and jiggling with every step. It looked so obscene I felt sick.

'Come on, Karen,' said Jack Hughes soothingly. 'Back into bed now.'

Karen turned on one bare foot and stared at him. Again, they were not her eyes. They looked fierce and bloodshot and powerful.

Jack Hughes came towards her with his hands held out. She backed away from him slowly with the same glare of hatred in her eyes. The hump on her back twisted and squirmed, like a sheep imprisoned in a sack.

'He – says – you – must – not—' she said haltingly, in her own voice.

Dr Hughes stopped. 'He says I must not *what*, Karen?'

She licked her lips. 'He – says – you – must – not – touch – him.'

'But Karen,' said Dr Hughes. 'If we don't look after you, he will not survive either. We are doing our best for *both* of you. We respect him. We want him to live.'

She backed further away, knocking a tray of instruments on to the floor.

'He – does – not – believe – you.'

'But why not, Karen? Haven't we done everything we can

to help? We're not soldiers, or warriors. We are medicine men, like himself. We want to help him.'

'He – is – in – pain.'

'In pain? Why?'

'It hurts – him. He – is – hurt.'

'Why is he hurt? What hurt him?'

'He – does – not – know. He – is – hurt. – It was – the light.'

'The light? What light?'

'He – will – kill – you – all—'

Karen suddenly started swaying. Then she screamed, and screamed, and dropped to her knees, clawing and clutching at her back. Michael and Wolf rushed up to her, and carried her swiftly back to bed. Jack Hughes fixed a hypodermic of tranquilizer, and shot it without hesitation into Karen's arm. Gradually, her cries diminished, and she sank into a nervous sleep, twitching and shaking and flickering her eyes.

'That settles it,' said Dr Hughes.

'Settles what, Jack?' I asked him.

'You and I are going straight to her parents and we're going to tell them exactly what's wrong. We're going to get that medicine man in from South Dakota and we're going to fight that beast until he's dead.'

'No guilt?' I asked. 'No sympathy?'

'Of course I have guilt, and I have sympathy, too. And it's because I have sympathy that I'm going to get it done.'

'I don't follow.'

'Harry,' said Jack, 'that medicine man is in *pain*. He didn't know why, but he said it was *the light*. If you know anything about gynecology, you'll know why we never X-ray foetuses unless we believe they are already dead, or they're a threat to their mother's lives. Every time a human being is X-rayed, the rays destroy cells in the area where the X-ray is directed. In an adult, that isn't too important, because they're fully developed, and the loss of a few cells isn't harmful. But in a tiny foetus, one cell destroyed can mean that a finger or a toe or even an arm or a leg will never develop.'

I stared at him. 'Do you mean that—'

'I simply mean that we've poured enough X-rays into that

85

medicine man to see through Fort Knox on a foggy day.'

I looked down at the vein-laced bulge that squirmed on Karen Tandys back. 'In other words,' I said, 'he's a monster. We've deformed him.'

Jack Hughes nodded. Outside, it was snowing again.

# CHAPTER FIVE

## DOWN IN THE GLOOM

I don't know what I expected a modern-day medicine man to look like, but Singing Rock could just as well have been an insurance salesman as a practitioner of ancient Indian magic. When I met him the next morning at La Guardia after his arrival from Sioux Falls, he was wearing a glossy grey mohair suit, his hair was short and shiny with oil, and there were heavy-rim spectacles on his less-than-hawklike nose.

He was dark-skinned, with black glittering eyes, and there were more wrinkles on his fifty-year-old face than you would expect on a white man, but otherwise he was as mundane and unspectacular as all the other businessmen on the flight.

I walked over to him and shook his hand. He only came up to my shoulder.

'Mr Singing Rock? My name's Harry Erskine.'

'Oh, hi. You don't have to call me *Mr* Singing Rock. Singing Rock on its own is okay. Was that a terrible flight? We had blizzards all the way. I thought we were going to have to put down in Milwaukee.'

'My car's outside,' I told him.

We collected his baggage and made our way to the car park. A watery sun was melting the slush, and there were the beginnings of a spring-like feeling around. A row of drips splashed on to the sidewalk from the terminus building, and one of them caught me on the neck.

I looked up. 'How come they don't hit *you*?' I asked.

'I'm a medicine man,' said Singing Rock urbanely. 'You think a drop of water would dare to hit me?'

I stowed his cases in the trunk, and we climbed into the car.

'Do you like the Cougar?' asked Singing Rock.

'It's pretty neat,' I said. 'I like it.'

'I have a green one,' he told me. 'I use it for fishing weekends. For work, I have a Marquis.'

'Oh,' I said. It didn't sound as though the medicine business was too bad down on the reservation these days.

As we drove out of La Guardia towards Manhattan, I asked Singing Rock how much he knew about the Karen Tandy case.

'I was told that some ancient medicine man was about to make a reappearance inside her body,' he said.

'And you don't find that hard to believe?'

'Why should I ... I've seen stranger things than that. Learning to escape into another time is pretty strong medicine, but there have been recorded cases of it happening. If you say it's true, and Dr Snow says it's true, then I'm inclined to believe that it's true.'

'You know this has got to be kept a strict secret?' I asked him, overtaking a truck, and switching on my windshield wipers to clear away the spray thrown up by its wheels.

'Of course. I wouldn't want to publicize it anyway. I have a steady investment business back in South Dakota, and I wouldn't want my clients to think I was reverting back to savagery.'

'You also know that this medicine man is extremely powerful?'

Singing Rock nodded. 'Any medicine man who can project himself through three centuries has got to be very powerful. I've been looking up the whole subject, and it appears that the greater the time-span the medicine man is able to cross, the more powerful his magic must be.'

'Did you find out anything more about it?'

'Not a great deal, but enough to give me a clear idea of what approach I'm going to have to take. You've heard of Gitche Manitou, the Great Spirit? Well, what we're dealing

with here is the spirit, or manitou, of this particular m[...]
cine man. He is obviously very strong, which means that
even in his previous lifetime in the 1650s, he was into his
fourth or fifth reincarnation. You see, each time a manitou
lives on earth as a human being, he gains more knowledge
and more strength. By the time he is into his seventh or
eighth reincarnation, he is ready to join Gitche Manitou for
ever as a permanent spirit. It's like graduation.'

I changed lanes. 'There's a similar kind of concept in
European spiritualism. What I want to know is, how do you
defeat a manitou like this?'

Singing Rock fished in his pocket for a small cigar and lit
it.

'I'm not saying it's easy,' he said. 'In fact, the whole
business is touch-and-go. But the basic principle is this.
Every magical spell, according to its strength, can be diverted. You can't nullify it. You can't stop it in its tracks. It has
its own spiritual momentum, and to arrest that momentum
would be like trying to stand in front of an express train. But
you can *divert* that express train and send it back the way it
came. All you need then is enough strength to alter its course
through three-hundred-and-sixty degrees.'

'It may be easier than you think,' I said. 'The doctors
made X-rays of this medicine man when he was still in a
foetal stage, and it looks as though they've deformed or injured him.'

'That won't make any difference,' said Singing Rock. 'The
spell was made when he was still whole and well, and that's
what counts.'

'Can you actually make him *leave* Karen Tandy?'

'I hope so. I don't think I'll have the power to divert
him right back to the 1650s. That would take a very strong
and experienced medicine man – somebody much more
powerful than me. But what I can do is get him out of her,
reverse the growth inside her, and redirect it to someone
else.'

I felt a chill. '*Someone else?* But you can't wish that on
someone else. What's the point of saving Karen Tandy's life
if we kill another person?'

back to my flat on Tenth Avenue, and he showered and drank coffee while I called up Karen's parents. I told them who I was, and they invited us over for lunch. I just hoped their food wouldn't stick in their throats when they heard what Singing Rock was suggesting.

We reached Mrs Karmann's apartment at one o'clock. The glazier had been around that morning, and the window that had been smashed during the seance was repaired. It was warm and expensive and cosy in there, but there was a distinctly awkward atmosphere.

Jeremy Tandy was a dry-looking, fair-haired man in his middle fifties. He wore a dark Nixonite suit, and his shirt was white and immaculate. His face had something of the elfishness of Karen, but it was matured and beaten into a harder and less compromising form.

His wife, Erica Tandy, was a light, slight woman with brown flowing hair and startlingly large eyes. She wore a black Dior suit, and contrasted it with simple gold jewellery. I was fascinated by her long gleaming finger-nails, and her $5,000 Piaget wristwatch.

Mrs Karmann was there, too, fussing around and trying to make everybody feel comfortable. She needn't have bothered. We all felt awkward and odd, and no amount of small talk could do anything about it.

'I'm Harry Erskine,' I said, wringing Jeremy Tandy's hand as firmly as I could. 'And this is Mr Singing Rock, from South Dakota. '

'Just Singing Rock will do,' said Singing Rock.

We sat down on chairs and settees, and Jeremy Tandy passed round cigarettes.

'Dr Hughes told me you had an interest in my daughter's case,' said Jeremy Tandy. 'But so far he hasn't told me who you are or what you do. Do you think you can enlighten me?'

I coughed. 'Mr Tandy – Mrs Tandy. A lot of what I'm going to say now will sound far-fetched. All I can tell you is that I was just as sceptical as you when I first found out about it. But the evidence is so overwhelming that everyone who knows anything about your daughter's illness has had to agree that this is *probably* – I won't say definitely – the cause of it.'

Step by step, I explained how Karen had come to me and told me about her dream. I told them how I had tracked down the Dutch ship, and how Amelia had raised the spirit of the medicine man. I told them about the reincarnation of medicine men, and our visit to Dr Snow in Albany. And then I told them about Singing Rock, and what he was going to try to do, and how much it would cost.

Jeremy Tandy listened to all this impassively. Every now and then he sipped at a glass of brandy, and he chain-smoked as he listened, but otherwise his face betrayed no sign of emotion.

When I'd finished, he sat back and looked at his wife. She seemed bewildered and confused, and I couldn't blame her. When you told it straight and cold, it was a pretty fantastic thing to swallow.

Jeremy Tandy leaned forward and looked me square in the eye.

'Is this a con?' he asked grittily. 'If it is, tell me right out now, and we'll let it go at that.'

I shook my head. 'Mr Tandy, I know it sounds incredible, but if you call Dr Hughes he will tell you the same story. And you have a cast-iron guarantee that it isn't a con. You don't have to pay any money at all until Karen is well. If she doesn't recover, that will mean that Singing Rock here has failed, and so he won't be needing the money anyway. If he fails, he may die.'

Singing Rock nodded soberly.

Jeremy Tandy stood up and paced the floor like a puma in a cage.

'My daughter's sick,' he snapped. 'They tell me she's dying. Then they tell me she's giving birth to a three-hundred-year-old medicine man. Then they tell me I'm going to need another medicine man to get rid of the first medicine man, and that's going to cost me thirty thousand bucks.'

He turned to me.

'Now is that bullshit, or is that bullshit?' he asked.

I tried not to lose my temper. 'Mr Tandy, I know it sounds

crazy. But why don't you just call Dr Hughes? Dr Hughes is a world expert on tumours. He knows more about tumours than I know about the New York subway, and I've been travelling on it since I was knee high to a high knee. Call him. Find out. But don't waste any time, because Karen is dying and as far as everyone can see there's only one way to save her.'

Jeremy Tandy stopped pacing, and stared at me with his head on one side.

'Do you really mean that you're not kidding?' he said.

'No, Mr Tandy, I am not kidding. I am serious. Ask Mrs Karmann here. She saw the face on the table, didn't you, Mrs Karmann?'

Mrs Karmann nodded. 'It's true, Jerry. I saw it with my own eyes. I trust Mr Erskine. He isn't lying.'

Mrs Tandy reached up and took her husband's hand. 'Jerry, darling, if it's the only way – we *must* do it.'

There was a long silence. Singing Rock brought out a handkerchief and blew his nose loudly. Somehow I never imagined that Indian medicine men needed handkerchiefs.

Finally, Jeremy Tandy threw up his hands.

'All right,' he said. 'You win. All I want is my daughter back again, sound and well, and if you can do that you can have *sixty*-thousand bucks.'

'Thirty is okay,' said Singing Rock, and when he said that, I think that Jeremy Tandy finally believed that the manitou was for real.

After lunch, I drove Singing Rock up to meet Dr Hughes at the Sisters of Jerusalem Hospital. Karen was under very heavy sedation, and there was a male nurse constantly at her bedside. Dr Hughes took us down to see her, and for the first time, Singing Rock saw exactly what he was up against. He stood at a respectful distance from the manitou, gazing at it above his surgical mask with worried eyes.

'Phew,' he said softly. 'That's something.'

Jack Hughes stood nervously beside him. 'What do you think, Singing Rock?'

'To quote a hackneyed line from old cowboy films, Dr

Hughes, this is heap powerful medicine. I've seen a lot of weird things – but this . . .'

'Come on,' said Jack, 'let's get out of here.'

We went back to his office and sat down. Singing Rock pulled a tissue from the box on Jack Hughes's desk and carefully mopped his forehead.

'Well,' said Jack. 'What's our plan of action?'

'The first thing I'd say is that we don't have long,' said Singing Rock. 'The way that manitou's growing, we'll need to be ready by tomorrow at the latest. What I'll have to do is mark out a magic circle around the bed, so that when the medicine man comes out, he can't cross it. That will hold him long enough to give me time to try and subjugate him with my own medicines. At least, I hope it will. It's quite possible that he's powerful enough to cross any magic circle I'm able to draw. I just don't know – and I won't know – until he actually appears. It depends on how much the X-rays have affected him. The original spell, the spell which he used to have himself reborn, is just as strong as he was able to make it in 1650. But any new spells he tries to cast may be hampered by what you've done to him. On the other hand, they may not. I can't count on it. They may have made him much more vengeful, and his magic more evil.'

Jack Hughes sighed. 'You don't sound very hopeful.'

'How can I be?' said Singing Rock. 'This is strictly David and Goliath. If I can hit him with a stone from my puny slingshot, I may be lucky and knock him out. But if I miss, then he's going to flatten me.'

'Is there anything you need?' I asked him. 'Any occult aids?'

Singing Rock shook his head. 'I brought all my goodies with me. If we can fetch my small suitcase out of your car, Harry, I could start right away by drawing the medicine circle. That will give us some protection, at least.'

Dr Hughes picked up the phone and asked for a porter. When the man arrived, he sent him down to my car in the basement, with instructions to collect Singing Rock's case.

'Whatever you do,' said Singing Rock, 'you mustn't disturb Karen Tandy's body when the medicine man has left

94

her. It mustn't be touched under any circumstances. If you disturb it even slightly, then the chances of her manitou being able to return to it and being revitalized will be practically nil.'

'Supposing the medicine man disturbs it himself . . .' I asked.

Singing Rock looked unhappy. 'If that happens, then we're probably wasting our time.'

Jack Hughes said: 'What I don't understand is why we can't just shoot him. He's a human being, after all, with normal flesh and blood.'

'That would defeat everything we've tried to do,' said Singing Rock. 'If you shoot him, his spirits will go to what the Indians used to call the Happy Hunting Grounds. His spirit, and Karen Tandy's spirit, and any other spirits he may have collected during his several lifetimes. If you kill him that way, then Karen Tandy will be gone for good. He possesses her manitou, and only he can release it. Voluntarily, or under duress.'

'And you don't think there's any chance of his releasing it voluntarily. . .' asked Jack Hughes.

'Not a hope,' said Singing Rock.

'And what do you think your chances are of being able to force it out of him?'

Singing Rock scratched his cheek thoughtfully. 'Three per cent,' he said. 'That's if I'm lucky.'

At that moment, the porter came up with the case. Singing Rock took it, laid it on Dr Hughes' desk, and opened it. As far as I could see, it was crammed with old hair and bones and packets of powder.

'Okay,' said the medicine man. 'Everything's here. Let's go down and draw the circle.'

We went downstairs again, and into Karen Tandy's private room. She was lying exactly as before, white-faced, with the swollen lump reaching almost down to her waist. Singing Rock didn't look at her, but busied himself taking powders and bones out of his case and laying them neatly on the floor.

'I want you to understand,' he said, 'that once I have

drawn this circle it must not be touched or disturbed in any way. You can cross it, but you must be extremely careful not to smudge it or break it. If it's even slightly broken, then it's useless.'

Dr Hughes said: 'Okay. I'll make sure that everyone who comes in here knows about that.'

Singing Rock went down on his hands and knees, and poured a circular track of red powder from a paper packet all the way around the bed. Then, inside it, he poured a circular track of white powder. At regular intervals he laid down dry white human bones, and spoke a soft incantation over each of them. Then he laid a garland of human hair all around the circle – old scalps from his tribe's historic totem.

'Gitche Manitou, protect me,' he prayed. 'Gitche Manitou, hear me and protect me.'

As he said these words, I felt a cold thrill slide down my back. Karen, on the bed, had opened one eye, and was staring fixedly across at Singing Rock with a quiet malevolence.

'Singing Rock,' I said gently, and pointed.

Singing Rock turned, and saw the single hate-filled eye. He licked his lips nervously, and then spoke to Karen in a quiet strained voice.

'Who are you?' he asked. 'Where do you come from?'

There was silence at first, but then Karen Tandy whispered hoarsely: 'I – am – much – mightier – than – you. Your – medicine – is – of – no – consequence – to – me. I – will – soon – slay – you – little – brother.'

'What is your name?' said Singing Rock.

'My – name – is – Misquamacus – I – will – soon – slay – you – little – brother – from – the – plains.'

Singing Rock stepped back nervously, staring at the single eye. Even when the eye dropped shut again, he was rubbing his hands in agitation against his surgical robe.

'What's the matter?' I asked him.

'It's *Misquamacus*,' he whispered, as though he were afraid of being overheard. 'He's one of the most notorious and powerful medicine men of all Indian history.'

'You've heard of him?'

'Anyone who knows anything about Indian magic has

heard of him. Even the Sioux knew about him way back before the white men came. He was considered to be the greatest of all medicine men, and he was in contact with manitous and demons that no other medicine man would dare to summon.'

'What does that mean?' said Jack Hughes anxiously. 'Does that mean you can't fight him?'

Singing Rock was sweating under the surgical face-mask. 'Oh, I can fight him, all right. But I don't give much for my chances of winning. Misquamacus was said to be able to control even the most ancient and wicked of Indian spirits. There were some manitous that were so old and evil that by the time the first white men arrived in America, they were only known in legend and stories by most tribes. But Misquamacus regularly called them for his own use. If he calls on them now, today, I just can't imagine what will happen.'

'But what can a spirit do?' I asked him. 'Can they actually hurt people who don't believe in them?'

'Of course,' explained Singing Rock. 'Just because you don't believe a tiger is going to maul you, that doesn't prevent it from doing so, does it? Once these manitous have been summoned into the physical world, they have physical powers and physical existence.'

'Holy Christ,' said Dr Hughes.

Singing Rock sniffed. '*He* won't help you. These demons have nothing to do with Christianity at all. You can fight Christian demons with crucifixes and holy water, but these demons will just laugh at you.'

'This circle,' I said, pointing to the ring of powder and bones. 'Do you think this will hold him?'

Singing Rock shook his head. 'I don't think so. Not for more than a few minutes, anyway. It might just give me the time to work a couple of spells on him, something to hold him down for longer. But Misquamacus was one of the greatest of circle-makers himself. He could draw circles that would hold back the most terrible spirits. This circle is the strongest one I'm capable of drawing, but he'll know how to break through that without any difficulty at all.'

'What I'm worried about is *Karen*,' said Jack Hughes. 'If

we're going to have a full-scale battle of wizards right here in her room, do you think she can possibly survive it?'

'Dr Hughes,' said Singing Rock, 'this is all-or-nothing. If I win this battle, then she will survive. If I don't, then I can't give you any guarantees about *who* will survive. With a medicine man as strong as Misquamacus, we might all of us die. You don't seem to understand what these manitous are. When I say they're powerful, I don't just mean they can knock a man over. If they're released from limbo without any control on them at all, they could wipe out this hospital, this whole block, this city.'

'Oh, come on, now,' said Dr Hughes.

Singing Rock made a last check of his medicine circle, and then led us out of Karen Tandy's room. In the corridor, we peeled off our face-masks and untied our robes.

'All I can say is – wait and see,' said Singing Rock. 'Now, I could use a meal and a beer. Is there anywhere to eat in this hospital?'

'Follow me,' said Jack Hughes. 'It's going to be a long night, so we might as well fuel up now.'

I checked the time. Five-o-five. By this time tomorrow, we would know whether we had won. If we hadn't, I couldn't even imagine what five-o-five on Tuesday evening would bring.

Lieutenant Marino of the NYPD was waiting for me in Dr Hughes' office when we got back from eating. He was sitting patiently with his hands in his lap, his black brush-cut hair sticking up like Mickey Spillane's before his weekly visit to the barber.

'Mr Erskine?' he said, rising to shake my hand.

I looked at him cautiously. 'Did you want something, lieutenant?'

'Oh, this and that. You must be Dr Hughes, sir,' he said to Jack. 'I'm Lieutenant Marino.' He flashed his badge.

'This is Singing Rock,' I said, introducing Singing Rock.

'Pleased to know you,' replied Lieutenant Marino. There was hand-shaking all round.

'Is there any problem?' I said.

'You could say that,' said Lieutenant Marino. 'Do you know two people called Amelia Crusoe and Stewart Mac-Arthur?'

'Of course, they're old friends of mine. What's the trouble?'

'They're dead,' said Lieutenant Marino. 'There was a fire in their apartment in the Village this morning, and they were both killed.'

I felt weird and trembly all over. I found a seat and sat down, and Dr Hughes fetched out his bottle of bourbon and poured me a glass. I swallowed a long mouthful. Lieutenant Marino passed me a cigarette, and lit it for me. When I spoke my voice was dry and croaky.

'God, that's terrible,' I said. 'How did it happen?'

'We don't know,' shrugged Marino. 'I was hoping that maybe you had some ideas about that.'

'What do you mean? What kind of ideas could I have about it? I've only just found out.'

Lieutenant Marino leaned forward confidentially. 'Mr Erskine, on Saturday morning, an old lady called Mrs Herz fell down a flight of steps and died. This is Monday. Two people are caught in a strange kind of flash fire in their apartment, and they die. All of these people have something in common. They're all friends of yours. Now, do you think I'm right to make a routine inquiry, or don't you?'

I sat back. My hands were shaking like two old men with the palsy.

'I guess you're right. But I have a witness who can tell you where I was this morning. I was up at La Guardia collecting Singing Rock here from his flight from South Dakota.'

'Is that true?' Lieutenant Marino asked Singing Rock.

Singing Rock nodded. He seemed to be thoughtful and preoccupied, and I wondered just what was turning over in his mind.

'Okay,' said Lieutenant Marino, standing up. 'That's all I wanted. I'm sorry I had to bring you such bad news.'

He got ready to leave, but Singing Rock held his arm.

'Lieutenant,' he said. 'Do you know what actually happened – with these two people?'

'It's hard to tell,' replied Marino. 'It seems as though the fire was instantaneous – more of a bomb than a fire. Both of the bodies were cindered up. We're checking for explosives now, but there wasn't any blast damage so I don't know whether we'll find any. It may have been some kind of freak electrical fault. We won't know for two or three days.'

'Okay, lieutenant,' said Singing Rock quietly. 'Thank you.'

Lieutenant Marino went to the door.

'Mr Erskine, I'd really appreciate it if you didn't leave town for a day or so. I'd like to know where to reach you in case there are any further inquiries.'

'Sure,' I told him softly. 'I'll be around.'

As soon as he'd gone, Singing Rock came over to me and laid his hand on my shoulder.

'Harry,' he said, 'I'm sorry. But now we know exactly what we're fighting against.'

'You don't think that . . .'

'No, I don't *think* it,' he said, 'I *know* it. Your friends annoyed Misquamacus by calling him up at that seance of yours. He probably only appeared to find out who it was that was daring to call him out of limbo. Misquamacus is quite capable of invoking fire like that. In plains' medicine, they used to call it the "lightning-that-sees", because it was completely selective. It only hit those people that the medicine man wanted to kill.'

Dr Hughes frowned. 'But Harry here was at that seance as well. Why hasn't Misquamacus done the same to him?'

'Because of *me*,' said Singing Rock. 'I may not be the greatest medicine man there ever was, but I am protected from simple sorcery like that by my amulets, and those who are friendly to me and who are around me will be protected as well. I imagine that because Misquamacus isn't properly reborn yet, he isn't able to work his full magic. I'm only guessing, of course.'

'I can hardly believe it,' said Jack Hughes. 'Here we are in a technological age, and a creature from four hundred years ago can destroy someone miles away in the Village with a flash of fire. What the hell is it all about?'

'It's about magic,' said Singing Rock. 'Real magic is created by the way that man uses his environment – the rocks, the trees, the water, the earth, the fire and the sky. And the spirits, too, the manitous. Today, we've forgotten how to call on all these things to help us. We've forgotten how to work real magic. But it can still be done. The spirits are still there, ready to be invoked. A century to a spirit is like a millisecond to us. They're immortal and patient, but they're also powerful and hungry. It takes a very strong man and a brave man to call them out of limbo. It takes an even stronger one to send them back there, and seal the gateway they came through.

'Do you know something, Singing Rock?' said Dr Hughes. 'The way you talk, you really give me the creeps.'

Singing Rock looked at him pragmatically. 'You have every reason to have the creeps. This is probably the creepiest thing that's ever happened.'

CHAPTER SIX

## BEYOND THE MISTS

Throughout Monday night, Singing Rock and I were to take it in turns to watch over Karen Tandy. We both agreed that Dr Hughes ought to go home and get a full night's sleep, because if we did manage to restore Karen's manitou to her body, then he would need to be as fit and fresh as possible to deal with any resuscitation that might be urgently needed.

We commandeered the hospital room next to Karen's, and while Singing Rock slept, I sat in the corridor on a hard chair, watching the window of our patient's firmly-closed door. There was a male nurse inside with her, in case she needed medical attention, but he had been warned that if he saw anything at all unusual, he was to bang on the door and call me.

I managed to find a copy of Dr Snow's book about the

Hidatsa Indians in the library, and I read it by the bald fluorescent hospital light. Most of it was pretty dry, but he was obviously well up on the sorcery of medicine men.

By two in the morning, my eyelids began to droop, and I began to feel as though there was nothing I wanted more than a hot shower, a stiff drink and ten hours of sack time. I twisted myself around in my chair to wake myself up a bit, but it wasn't long before a relaxed and cloudy feeling started to seep over me again.

Without realizing it, I began to doze, and as I dozed, I began to dream. I dreamed I was surrounded by a warm and slippery darkness, but it wasn't claustrophobic or suffocating. It felt womb-like and comfortable, and it was giving me strength and nourishment. I felt as if I was waiting for something to happen – waiting for the right moment. When that moment came, I would have to slide out of this warm darkness into some chilly and unknown place. Somewhere frightening and alien.

The feeling of fear woke me up. I immediately looked at my watch to see how long I'd been asleep. Not more than five or ten minutes, I guessed. I stood up and went over to the window of Karen Tandy's room. She was still lying there, covered by a loose sheet, which hid most of the hideous bulge on her back. She was still unconscious, and her face was yellow and almost skull-like. Her eyes were circles with purple shadows, and there were deep drawn lines on her cheeks. She looked as though she were on the verge of death. Only the flickering needles of the electric diagnosis machines beside her bed showed that something was still alive inside her body.

The male nurse, Michael, sat cross-legged reading a science fiction paperback called *Girl from Green Planet*. I would gladly have traded it for my academic tome of the lifestyle of the Hidatsas.

I went back to my bony chair and sat down. Singing Rock was due to relieve me at 3 a.m., and I couldn't wait. I smoked and twiddled my thumbs. That time of night, you feel that the whole world is empty, and you're on your own in some strange secret time – a time when pulse-rates slur and fade, and deep breathing takes you diving down into a bottomless well of monstrous dreams and nightmares.

I finished my cigarette, ground it out, and checked my watch again. It was two-thirty. Evening was long past, and morning was still a long way ahead. Somehow, the idea of facing Misquamacus by night was much more frightening than the thought of facing him by day. At night, you feel that evil spirits are much more readily to call, and that even shadows, or the odd shape of your clothes across the back of a chair, can take on a sinister life of their own.

When I was a child, I used to be terrified to go out to the bathroom in the middle of the night, because it meant passing by the open sitting-room door. I was frightened that one night, when the moonlight was slanting in through the venetian blinds, I would see people sitting silent and stiff in the chairs. Not blinking, not moving, not speaking. Previous occupants, long dead, relaxing stiffly in the chairs that were once theirs.

I had that same feeling now. I kept glancing down the long and empty corridor, to see if some blurry shape were moving in the distance. I looked at all the doors, to see if any of them were easing slowly open. Night is the province of magic and magicians, and my Tarot cards had warned me about night and death and men who worked evil wonders. Now I was facing the threat of all three of them.

At two-forty-five I lit another cigarette and puffed the smoke softly into the total silence of the empty corridor. By now, even the elevators had stopped running and the feet of the night-staff were muffled by the thick plush carpets. For all I knew, I could be totally alone in the whole world. Every time I shifted my feet, I frightened myself.

Tired as I was, I began to wonder whether the whole situation was truly real, or whether I was dreaming it, or imagining it. Yet if Misquamacus didn't exist, how did I know his name, and what was I doing here, keeping up this lonely vigil in a hospital corridor? I smoked, and tried to read Dr Snow's book a little more, but my eyes were too blurry with exhaustion, and I gave up.

It must have been the soft squeaking of skin on glass that

made me look up at the window of Karen Tandy's room right then. It was a tiny, almost imperceptible sound, like someone cleaning silver spoons in another part of the house. *Squeak, squikkkkk . . .*

I jumped with shock. There was a *face* pressed against the window, with horribly contorted features. Its eyes bulged and its teeth were bared in a stretched, silent howl.

It was only there for a second, and then there was a slushy, spraying sound, and the whole window was obliterated with blood. A spout of thick red pumped from the keyhole, and ran down the outside of the door.

'Singing ROCCCKKKK!' I yelled, and burst into the next-door room where he was sleeping. I banged on the light, and he was sitting up, his face crumpled with sleep, his eyes wide with expectancy and fear.

'What's happened?' he snapped, rolling out of bed and pushing quickly out of the room into the corridor.

'There was a *face* there – at the window – just for a second. Then there was nothing but all this blood.'

'He's out,' said Singing Rock. 'Or nearly. That must have been the male nurse you saw at the window.'

'The nurse? But what the hell has Misquamacus done to him?'

'Old Indian magic. He's probably invoked the spirits of the body, and turned him inside-out.'

'*Inside-out?*'

Singing Rock ignored me. He went swiftly back to his room, and opened up his suitcase. He took out beads and amulets, and a leather bottle full of some liquid. One of the amulets, a fierce green copper face on a rawhide thong, he hung around my neck. He sprinkled some reddish powder over my hair and shoulders, and touched me above the heart with the tip of a long white bone.

'Now you're reasonably protected,' he said. 'At least you won't end up like Michael.'

'Listen, Singing Rock,' I said. 'I think we ought to have a gun. I know that it would kill Karen Tandy if we shot Misquamacus, but as a last resort, we might have to.'

Singing Rock shook his head firmly. 'No. If we shot

Misquamacus, we would have his manitou pursuing us in vengeance for the rest of our lives. The only way we can defeat him for ever is through magic. That way, he can never return. And anyway, in any kind of sorcery, a gun is more dangerous to the person who uses it than it is to the person who's being fired at. Now come on, we don't have much time to lose.'

He led me back to the door of Karen Tandy's room. The blood had thinned on the window now, but all we could see inside was the dim glow of the bedside light, scarlet through the gore.

'Gitche Manitou, protect us. Gitche Manitou, protect us,' muttered Singing Rock, and turned the door handle.

There was something wet and messy behind the door, and Singing Rock had to push hard to slide it all out of the way. There was a nauseating smell of vomit and faeces, and my feet skidded on the floor as I stepped in. Michael's remains were lying in a raw red bubbly heap, strung with pipes and veins and intestines, and I could only glance at it. I felt as if I was going to puke.

There was blood spattered everywhere – all over the walls and the bedsheets and the floor. In the middle of this gory chaos lay Karen Tandy, and she was wriggling under her coverings – wriggling like a huge white bug trying to work its way out of a chrysalis.

'It's very soon,' whispered Singing Rock. 'She must have been struggling and Michael went to help her. That's why Misquamacus killed him.'

Forcing my stomach to stop heaving, I watched in horrified fascination as the enormous bulge on Karen Tandy's back began to heave and twist. It was so large now that her own body seemed like nothing more than a papery carnival ghost, and her thin arms and legs were flopped about by the fierce squirming of the beast that was being born on her back.

'Gitche Manitou, give me power. Bring me the spirits of darkness and power. Gitche Manitou, hear my call to you,' muttered Singing Rock. He traced complicated patterns in the air with his long magic bones, and threw powders all around. The scent of dried herbs and flowers mingled with the vivid stench of blood.

I suddenly had a singing, metallic sensation in my head, like breathing nitrous oxide at the dentist. The whole scene seemed peculiarly unreal, and I felt detached and strange, as though I were looking through my eyes from the darkness of some other place. Singing Rock grasped my arm, and only then did the feeling begin to fade.

'He's casting spells already,' whispered the medicine man. 'He knows we're here and he knows we're going to try and fight him. He will do many strange things to your mind. He will try and make you feel as though you do not really exist, like he did just then. He will also try and make you feel afraid, and suicidal, and desperately alone. He has the power to do all that. But these are only tricks. What we must really look out for are the manitous that he summons, because they are almost unstoppable.'

Karen Tandy's body was thrown this way and that across the bed. She was dead already, I thought, or almost dead. Her mouth opened every now and then and she gave a little gasp, but that was only because the wriggling medicine man on her back was pressing against her lungs.

Singing Rock caught hold of my arm. 'Look,' he said quietly.

The white skin at the upper part of the bulge was being pressed from inside, as if by a finger. The finger worked harder and harder against it, trying to claw its way through. I stood frozen, and I could hardly feel my legs. I thought I might collapse at any moment. I watched, almost without seeing it at all, as the finger squirmed and wriggled in a desperate effort to break out.

A long nail pierced the skin, and a watery yellow fluid suddenly gushed from the hole, streaked with blood. There was a rich, foetid smell, like decaying fish. The sac of Karen Tandy's back sank and emptied as the birth fluid of Misquamacus poured out of it on to the sheets.

'Call Dr Hughes – get him here as quick as you can,' said Singing Rock.

I went to the phone on the wall, wiped the blood off it

with my handkerchief, and dialled the switchboard. When she answered, the girl's voice seemed so blank and unconcerned that she seemed to be speaking from another world.

'This is Mr Erskine. Can you get Dr Hughes up to Miss Tandy's room – as soon as you can. Tell him it's *started*, and it's *urgent*.'

'Okay, sir.'

'Call him right away. Thank you.'

'You're welcome.'

I turned back to the hideous birth struggle on the bed. From the slit in the skin, a dark hand had emerged, and was tearing a larger and larger hole in the bulge with a sound like ripping plastic.

'Can't you do anything *now*,' I whispered to Singing Rock. 'Can't you put a spell on him before he gets out of there?'

'No,' said Singing Rock. He was very calm, but I could see by the strain on his face that he was also very frightened. He held his bones and his powders ready, but his hands were trembling.

A long tear, about three feet deep, had now appeared in Karen Tandy's back. Her own face now lay pale and dead against the bed, smothered in clotted blood and sticky fluid. I couldn't believe that there was any way to revive her now. She seemed so mutilated and torn, and the thing that was coming out of her seemed so strong and evil.

Another hand emerged from the rip in her flesh, and the skin was parted wide. Slowly, greasily, a head and shoulders rose from the hole, and I felt a deep dark chill when I saw the same hard face that had appeared on the cherrywood table. It was Misquamacus, the ancient medicine man, coming alive again in a new world.

His long black hair was flattened against his broad skull with oil and fluid. His eyes were stuck closed, and his coppery skin glistened with the fetid muck of his womb. His cheekbones were high and flat, and his prominent hooked nose was occluded with foetal fats. Strings of mucus hung from his lips and chin.

Both Singing Rock and I stood totally silent as Misquamacus peeled Karen's flaccid skin away from his bare greasy torso. Then the medicine man raised himself on his hands, and worked his hips free. His genitals were puffy and swollen, the same way that a boy child's are at birth, but there was dark pubic hair smeared against his scarred belly.

Misquamacus heaved one leg out, with a sickening suction sound, like pulling a rubber boot out of thick mud. Then the other leg.

And it was now that we saw what damage the X-rays had done to him. Instead of full muscular legs, his lower limbs both ended above the knee, in tiny deformed club feet, with pulpy dwarfish toes. Modern technology had crippled the medicine man in his womb.

Gradually, with his eyes still tight shut, Misquamacus lifted himself away from Karen Tandy's torn body. He gripped the rail of the bed to support himself, and sat there with his stunted little legs sucking air into his fluid-filled lungs, and letting the creamy phlegm run from the side of his mouth.

All I wished at that moment was that I had a gun, and could blow this monstrosity to pieces, and have it over with. But I had seen enough of his occult power to know that I wouldn't be doing myself any favours. Misquamacus was capable of haunting me for the rest of my life, and when I died his manitou would have horrible revenge on mine.

'I will need your support,' said Singing Rock quietly. 'With each spell I cast, I will want you to concentrate deeply on its success. With two of us here, we might just succeed in holding him down.'

As if he had been listening, the crippled Misquamacus slowly opened one yellow eye, and then the other, and looked across at us with a chilling mixture of curiosity, contempt and hatred.

He then looked down at the floor, and saw the medicine circle around the bed, with its red and white powders and its bones.

'Gitche Manitou,' said Singing Rock loudly. 'Hear me now, and send your power to my aid.'

He began to shuffle and dance, and make patterns in the

air with his bones. I tried to do as he had asked me, and concentrate on making the spell work. But it was hard to take my eyes away from the cold and passive creature on the bed, who was staring at us with total vindictiveness.

'Gitche Manitou,' chanted Singing Rock, 'send your messengers with locks and keys. Send your jailers and your guards. Hold down this spirit, imprison Misquamacus. Shut him up with bars and with chains. Freeze his mind and stay his sorcery.'

He then went into a long Indian invocation that I could hardly follow, but I stood there and prayed and prayed that his magic would work, and that the medicine man on the bed would be trapped by spiritual forces.

But a weird feeling began to penetrate my mind – a feeling that what we were doing was puny and useless, and that the best thing we could do would be to leave Misquamacus alone, leave him to do whatever he wanted to do. He was much stronger than us, he was so much wiser. It seemed to me then that it was futile to continue to battle against him, because he would only have to summon one of his Indian demons, and we would both meet a horrible death.

'Harry,' gasped Singing Rock. *Don't let him into your mind.* Help me – I need your help!'

I made an effort to shrug off the pall of hopelessness that was seeping through my brain. I turned to Singing Rock, and I saw sweat running down his face, and deep lines of strain and anxiety carved into his cheeks.

*'Help me, Harry, help me!'*

I stared at the dark, hideous creature on the bed and I concentrated every ounce of my will into paralyzing him. He stared back at me with those glassy yellow eyes, as if daring me to defy him, but I tried to ignore my terror and pin him down with sheer mental effort. *You are helpless*, I thought. *You cannot move, you cannot work your magic.*

But, inch by inch, Misquamacus began to work himself off the bed. He kept his eyes on both of us all the time. Singing Rock was throwing powders and beating his bones, but Misquamacus seemed unaffected by everything that he was doing. The medicine man dropped himself heavily to the floor, and crouched on his ghastly little legs within the magic circle, his face a mask of impassive hate.

Painfully, using his hands to swing himself along like an ape, Misquamacus approached the circle. If that doesn't hold him, I thought, I am going to be out of that door and half-way to Canada before you can say cold-blooded cowardice.

Singing Rock's voice grew shriller and shriller. 'Gitche Manitou, hold Misquamacus away from me!' he called. 'Keep him within the circle of charms! Lock and chain him!'

Misquamacus paused, and stared balefully around at the medicine circle. For a moment, I thought he was going to heave himself straight across it, and launch himself towards us. But then he paused, and settled back on his hips, and closed his eyes again. Singing Rock and I stood silent for one breathless moment, and then Singing Rock said: 'We've held him.'

'You mean he can't get out?'

'No, he can get across it all right. But not yet. He hasn't the strength. He's resting to get it back.'

'But how long is he going to need? How long do we have?'

Singing Rock looked warily at the hunched naked form of Misquamacus.

'It's impossible to say. It might be a few minutes, it might be a few hours. I think I've called enough spiritual interference down to give us thirty or forty minutes anyway.'

'What now?'

'We'll just have to wait. As soon as Dr Hughes gets here, I think we ought to have this floor of the hospital evacuated. He's going to wake up before long, and then he's going to be angry and vengeful and almost impossible to deal with, and I don't want innocent people hurt.'

I checked the time. 'Jack should be here at any minute. Listen, do you really think we shouldn't have a few guns?'

Singing Rock wiped his face. 'You're a typical white American. You've been brought up on a diet of TV Westerns and Highway Patrol, and you think that the gun is the answer to everything. Do you want to save Karen Tandy or not?'

'Do you seriously think she can be saved? I mean – just look at her.'

The limp, shrivelled form of Karen Tandy's body was lying awkwardly and emptily across the bed. I could hardly recognize her as the same girl who had come into my flat only four nights before, telling me about her dreams of ships and moonlit coasts.

Singing Rock said softly: 'According to the lore of Indian magic, she can still be saved. If there's a chance, I think we ought to try.'

'You're the witch doctor.'

At that moment, Dr Hughes and Wolf, the other male nurse came clattering down the corridor. They took one look at the blood, and at the silent form of Misquamacus, and stepped back in horror.

'God,' said Jack Hughes shakily. 'What the hell happened?'

We stepped out of the room and into the corridor with him.

'He killed Michael,' I said. 'I was sitting here when it happened. It was too quick to do anything about it. Then he forced his way out of Karen. Singing Rock thinks we've held him for a while with the medicine circle, but we don't have long.'

Dr Hughes bit his lips. 'I think we ought to call the police. I don't care what century that thing is from, he's murdered enough people.'

Singing Rock firmly protested. 'If we call the police, he will only kill them as well. Bullets can't solve this problem, Dr Hughes. We've decided to play this game a particular way, and now we're stuck with it. Only magic can help us now.'

'Magic,' said Dr Hughes bitterly. 'To think I'd end up using *magic*.'

'Singing Rock thinks we ought to evacuate this floor of the hospital,' I said. 'Once Misquamacus wakes up, he's going to use everything he's got to get his revenge on us.'

'There's no need,' said Dr Hughes. 'This is a surgical and operating floor only. We had Karen down here so that she could be nearer the theatre. There are no other patients on ten. All I have to do is tell the rest of the staff to stay away.'

We dragged some more chairs into the corridor and sat down, keeping a watchful eye on the motionless bulk of Misquamacus. Wolf went up to Dr Hughes' office and came back with a couple of bottles of bourbon, and we revived ourselves. It was three-forty-five, and we still had a long night ahead of us.

'Now that he's emerged,' said Dr Hughes, 'how are we going to deal with him? How are we going to make him give up Karen Tandy's manitou?' I could tell he was embarrassed about using the Indian word for spirit.

'The way I see it,' said Singing Rock, 'we have to convince Misquamacus somehow that he's in a hopeless situation, which he is. Although he is very powerful, he's an anachronism. Magic and sorcery may be dangerous, but in a world where people don't believe in it, they have very limited uses. Even if Misquamacus kills all of us – even if he kills everyone in this hospital – what's he going to do in the outside world? He's physically crippled, he's completely unversed in contemporary culture and science, and one way or another, he will just be overwhelmed. Even if it doesn't happen right here, somebody's going to put a bullet in him sooner or later.'

'But how are you going to convince him?' I asked Singing Rock.

'I guess the only way is to *tell* him,' said Singing Rock. 'One of us will have to open up his mind to Misquamacus, and give him a mental tour of what the modern world is really like.'

'Won't he think that's just a magical trap? A bluff?' asked Dr Hughes.

'Possibly. But I don't see what else we can do.'

'Wait a minute,' said Dr Hughes, turning to me. 'Something just occurred to me. You remember when you told me about Karen Tandy's dream, Harry – the one about the ship and the coast and all that stuff?'

'Yes, of course.'

'Well, what strikes me about that dream is that there was

so much *fear* in it. Misquamacus was *afraid* of something. And it was obviously something that was terrifying enough to make him risk this whole business of swallowing burning oil and being reborn. Now, what do you think he could have been afraid off?'

'That's a good point,' I said. 'What do you think, Singing Rock?'

'I don't know,' said the Sioux. 'He might simply have been afraid of death at the hands of the Dutch. Just because their manitous go on living in limbo after death, that doesn't mean that medicine men aren't concerned about being killed. And there are ways of killing medicine men so that their manitous can never return to the earth. Maybe the Dutchmen knew how to do it, and threatened him.'

'That still doesn't make sense,' said Dr Hughes. 'We've seen already how Misquamacus can defend himself. No Dutchman could have gotten close enough to harm him. Yet he was still frightened. Now, why? What did the Dutch have in the seventeenth century that could have terrified a medicine man like Misquamacus?'

'I guess they had guns,' said Wolf. 'The Indians didn't have guns, did they?'

'That wouldn't fit,' replied Singing Rock. 'Misquamacus is powerful enough to resist guns. You saw what he did to Harry's friends, with the lightning-that-sees. You would only have to point a gun at him, and he could blow it up in your hand.'

'The Dutch were Christians,' I suggested. 'Do you think there's anything in the Christian religion which could have exorcized Misquamacus' demons and manitous?'

'No way,' Singing Rock said. 'There is nothing in Christianity to equal the power of the old Indian spirits.'

Dr Hughes was frowning deeply, as though he were trying to remember something he'd heard about years and years ago. Then suddenly he snapped his fingers.

'*I know*,' he said. 'There *was* something very important which the Dutch settlers had which the Indians didn't. Something which threatened the Indians, and which they had never come across before, and couldn't fight.'

'What was that?' I asked him.

'*Disease*,' said Jack Hughes. 'The Dutchmen brought all kinds of viruses that were unknown on the North American continent. Especially influenza viruses. Whole tribes were wiped out by European diseases, because they had no antibodies, and couldn't resist even the simplest colds and flu. And the medicine men couldn't help them, because they had no sorcery which could work against something they knew nothing at all about. Invisible, deadly and quick. If you ask me, that's what Misquamacus was afraid of. The Dutch were destroying his tribe with a medicine he couldn't see or understand.'

Singing Rock looked excited. 'That's inspired, Dr Hughes. That is really inspired.'

'One thing, though,' I interjected. 'Surely Misquamacus would now be immune to influenza? If he's been born in anything like the way a normal baby is born, he would have gotten antibodies from Karen Tandy's bloodstream.'

'No, I don't think so,' said Dr Hughes. 'His nervous system was intertwined with Karen's, but their bloodstreams weren't connected in the same way that a foetus is connected to its mother. The energy he was drawing from her was electrical energy from her brain cells and spinal system, there was no actual intermingling in the usual physical sense.'

'That means,' said Singing Rock, 'that we could give our medicine man a dose of the grippe. Or threaten to.'

'Certainly,' said Dr Hughes. 'Hold on just a moment.'

He went to the wall telephone and dialled quickly.

'Put me through to Dr Winsome,' he said, when the switchboard answered.

Singing Rock took a look at the silent shape of Misquamacus, hunched and sinister on the floor of Karen Tandy's blood-smeared room. Somehow the thought of giving this creature the influenza didn't seem like a very effective answer. But, apart from Singing Rock's sorcery, we didn't have very much else to turn to.

'Dr Winsome?' said Jack Hughes. 'Look, I'm sorry to wake you up, but I have an urgent problem here, and I badly need some virus samples.'

There was a pause while Dr Hughes listened to the tinny voice on the other end of the phone.

'Yes, I know it's four o'clock in the morning, Dr Winsome, but I wouldn't have called you if it hadn't have been desperate. That's right. I need influenza virus. Well, how soon can you get down here?'

He listened some more, and then hung up the phone.

'Dr Winsome is coming right away. He has enough influenza virus in his laboratory to bring down the whole population of Cleveland, Ohio.'

'Maybe he ought to try it sometime,' said Singing Rock, with unexpected humour.

It was now four-o-five, and Misquamacus hadn't stirred. All four of us stayed in the corridor, keeping a close watch on his dark, troll-like body, although we were all exhausted by now, and the stench of Michael's corpse was almost overpowering.

'What's it like outside?' I asked Dr Hughes.

'Cold. Snowing again,' he told me. 'I hope Dr Winsome doesn't have any trouble getting here.'

Another half-hour passed. It would soon be dawn. We sat huddled on our chairs, wearily rubbing our eyes and smoking to keep ourselves awake. Only sheer nervous tension kept me from nodding off. I hadn't slept since Sunday night, and then I had only had four or five hours.

At four-forty-five, we heard a rustling noise from inside Karen Tandy's room. We looked up quickly. Misquamacus still had his eyes closed, but he appeared to be stirring. Singing Rock got to his feet and picked up his bones and powders.

'I think he's waking,' he said. There was a shake in his voice. This time, he knew that the ancient wonder-worker would have almost all his sorcerer's powers restored. He stepped softly into Karen Tandy's room, and we followed him, and stood behind him to give him support.

Slowly, Misquamacus stretched his hard muscular arms, scarred with magical patterns. He raised his head, with his eyes still shut, so that it was facing directly at us.

'Is he awake?' whispered Jack Hughes.

'I don't know,' said Singing Rock. 'But he will be soon.'

Suddenly, we heard a breathy noise from the bed. The blue-white lips of Karen Tandy's body seemed to be moving, and air was hissing in and out of them.

'She's still *alive*,' said Wolf.

'No,' said Singing Rock. 'Misquamacus is doing that. I think he's going to speak to us through her, like he did before. He's using her like a microphone, so that he can talk to us in our own language.'

'But that's *impossible*,' protested Jack Hughes. 'He's nowhere near her.'

'It might be scientifically impossible,' said Singing Rock quietly. 'But this is not science. This is Indian magic.'

We stood stock-still as deeper breaths began to hiss and gurgle from Karen Tandy's throat. Then she began to whisper to us, in a faint hollow voice that froze every nerve in my body.

'You – have – tried – to – defy – me – hissssss,' breathed the voice. 'You – have – hurt – me – and – I – am – feeling – great – pain. I – intend – to – punish – you – for – that – sssssssss.'

Her dead lungs collapsed, and her lips stopped quivering. We turned back to look at Misquamacus himself. His yellowy eyes suddenly opened, and stared at us with glittering malevolence. The same smile that had tightened his face when he appeared on the cherrywood table crossed his expression now.

Singing Rock started his incantations, and tapped his bones in a soft, knocking rhythm. But we could tell that his sorcery was nothing compared to that of Misquamacus, because the neon lights in the room began to flicker and fade, and within a few seconds we were plunged into complete darkness.

I stretched my arms out, trying to take a friendly hand, but I couldn't seem to reach anyone. I was terrified in case I touched the still-slimy face of Misquamacus.

'*Don't move*,' hissed Singing Rock, with fright in his voice. '*Don't anybody move.*'

But *somebody*, or *something* was moving in the room, and it was shuffling towards us with a slow, irresistible gait.

# CHAPTER SEVEN

## PAST THE DUSK

Wolf struck his cigarette-lighter, and turned the gas up full, and the tall yellow flame lit the room in a carousel of hideous shadows.

Misquamacus, with an animal grin on his glistening face, was still crouched within the medicine circle, but just in front of him, on the floor, the red and white powders that Singing Rock had set down were shifting and sliding apart, like iron filings drawn away by a magnet.

'He's breaking it!' shouted Jack Hughes. 'Singing Rock – for God's sake!'

Singing Rock took a step forward and stood right in front of Misquamacus – only a couple of feet away from the deformed medicine man, and with only the rapidly-dispersing powders of the medicine circle between them.

He cast more powders at Misquamacus, and drew signs in the air with his bones, but Misquamacus simply twitched and flinched, as though he were batting away midges. From Karen Tandy on the bed, we heard a soft and hideous laugh, dying away in a bellows-like hiss.

The last of the medicine circle slithered away, and now there was nothing between us and the hell-bent Misquamacus. I didn't know whether to stay put or run, but I knew that Singing Rock needed all of us badly to support his sorcery, and so I stayed where I was, tingling with fear.

The naked Misquamacus raised himself as tall as he could on his stunted legs, and spread his arms wide. Out of his own lips, in a harsh and guttural voice, came a long Indian incantation, repetitive and involved, and then with one bony hand he pointed across the room.

I followed the line of his finger. He was pointing directly at the gory corpse of Michael, the male nurse.

Singing Rock stepped back quickly. 'Get out of here, *now!*' he snapped, and pushed us towards the door.

Just as I got out into the corridor, I saw something that literally started my teeth chattering. The bloody heap of Michael's body was *moving*: exposed arteries were pulsing, naked nerves were throbbing, and his inside-out lungs, like two dripping balloons, were drawing breath again.

By the feeble orange light of Wolf's cigarette-lighter we saw the shambles of Michael's body rise gorily to its feet. Deep in the bleeding tissue of the inverted face, two watery eyes stared out at us – squid's eyes, from a terrible submarine nightmare.

Then step by liquid step, leaving behind it a trail of viscous membrane, Michael's corpse started to walk towards us, smearing everything it touched with blood.

'Oh, Christ,' said Jack Hughes, in a desperate, horrified voice.

But Singing Rock was not idle. He fumbled in his pocket for his leather bottle, unstoppered it, and poured some of its contents into the palm of his hand. With wide, sweeping strokes, he sprayed a pattern of magical liquid into the air, across and over the shambling wreck of Michael's body.

'Gitche Manitou, take life from this creature,' he muttered. 'Gitche Manitou, reward this servant with death.'

Michael's body sagged, and dropped to its knees, bare muscles sliding over exposed bones. It finally collapsed, and lay in a heap beside the door.

Inside the room, Misquamacus was at work again. We couldn't see him now, because Wolf's cigarette-lighter flame was rapidly sinking, but we would hear him chanting and talking and tossing the bones and hair that Singing Rock had used to make his medicine circle.

'Wolf,' said Singing Rock. 'Go and fetch us a few flash-lights. We must be able to see what we're doing. Misquamacus can see in the dark, and it's easier for him to summon his demons in the dark. Please – as quick as you can!'

Wolf handed me his hot cigarette-lighter, with its bead of diminishing flame, and ran down the corridor to the elevators. He almost didn't make it. As he turned the corner, there was a blue-white flash of dazzling fire. It sent sparks crawling across the floor, and left a searing orange after-image on my eyes.

'Wolf!' called Singing Rock. 'Are you okay?'

'Okay, sir!' shouted back Wolf. 'I'll be right back!'

'What the hell was that?' said Jack Hughes.

'The lightning-that-sees,' said Singing Rock. 'That was what killed your friends, Harry. I thought Misquamacus would try to get him like that once he was away from me, so I diverted it.'

'It still went damn close,' said Jack.

'A miss is as good as a mile,' I commented. The lighter had almost dwindled away now, and I was straining my eyes to see what was happening in Karen Tandy's room. I could hear shufflings and bumpings, but it was impossible to make anything out.

Darkness enveloped us again. We kept a hand on each other's shoulders, so that we wouldn't be separated. It also helped to concentrate the force of Singing Rock's spells, whenever he cast them. With complete blackness pressing against our eyes, we kept our ears pricked up for the slightest sound.

After a few moments, we heard Misquamacus chanting again.

'What's he doing?' whispered Dr Hughes.

'Something I was afraid of,' said Singing Rock. 'He's summoning an Indian demon.'

'A *demon*?' asked Jack.

'Not exactly a demon in European terms. But the Indian equivalent. One of the ancient ones.'

'Do you know which one he's calling?' I said.

Singing Rock listened to the coarse, muttering incantation as closely as he could.

'I don't know. He's using a name from his own tribal language. Although the demons are all the same throughout North America, each tribe has a different name for them. This one is something called Kahala, I think, or K'malah. I'm not sure.'

'How can you fight it if you don't know which one it is?' I said.

I could imagine Singing Rock's lined lugubrious face.

'I can't. I'll have to wait and see when it appears.'

Clinging together, we waited for the ancient apparition to manifest itself. Through the darkness, we saw pale flickers of greenish light coming from Karen Tandy's room, and coils of pallid smoke.

'Is the place on *fire*?' asked Dr Hughes.

'No,' said Singing Rock. 'The manitou is being formed out of that smoke. It's like ectoplasm, you know, in European spiritualism.'

The green light faded, and then we heard more noises from inside the room. There was a sound like *scaly claws scratching the floor*, and then we heard Misquamacus talking. He spoke for at least a couple of minutes, and then, to my horror, I heard someone talking back to him. Someone who spoke in a grating, unearthly voice – guttural and cruel.

'He's telling the demon to destroy us,' said Singing Rock. 'Now, whatever you do, keep hold of each other, and don't try to run. If you run, you'll be out of my protection, and he'll get you.'

Two lines from *The Ancient Mariner* suddenly pounded through my brain – about the man who looks back and then no longer turns his head *'because he knows a fearful fiend doth close behind him tread.'*

The scraping of claws on the floor of Karen Tandy's room began to move towards us. Through the gloom, I began to make out a tall dark shadow standing in the doorway, facing us across the corridor. It seemed to be like a man, and yet completely unlike a man. I squinted into the darkness, and made out things that looked like claws and scales.

'What is it . . ?' hissed Jack Hughes.

'It's the demon we called Lizard-of-the-Trees,' said Singing Rock. 'He is the evil manitou of forests and woods and all trees. I think that Misquamacus has chosen him because he knows I am from the plains, and I have less control over the manitous of the forest.'

The dark being in the doorway started to move towards us, uttering a thin insect-like piping in its throat. Singing Rock immediately cast powders and liquid at it, and rattled his magic bones.

It could only have been two or three feet away when it stopped.

'You've done it,' said Jack. 'You've stopped it.'

'It won't kill us, because my medicine is too strong for it,' Singing Rock said breathlessly. 'But it refuses to return to limbo without a sacrifice.'

'A *sacrifice*? What the hell does it want?'

'A small piece of living flesh, that's all.'

I said: '*What??* But how can we give it that?'

'Anything,' said Singing Rock. 'A finger, an ear.'

'You can't be serious,' I said.

'It won't leave without it,' Singing Rock replied. 'And I can't hold it back for very much longer. It's either that, or we'll be torn to shreds. I mean that. This creature has a beak, like an octopus, or a pterodactyl. It can rip you open like a sack of beans.'

'All right,' said Dr Hughes quietly. '*I'll* do it.'

Singing Rock took a deep breath. 'Thank you, Dr Hughes. It should be quite quick. Stretch your hand out towards it. Give it your little finger. Fold all the rest of your fingers right back. I will try and keep most of your hand within the circle of my spell. Once it's bitten, take your hand away at once. As quickly as you can. You don't want it to take any more.'

I could feel Dr Hughes shaking as he reached out his hand towards the shadowy bulk of the Lizard of the Trees. I heard razor-like claws scraping on the floor as he stretched nearer and nearer, and that thin piping sound as the demon breathed.

There was a horrible excited rustle, and the claws skidded frantically on the corridor floor, and then a crunch like I never want to hear again.

'*Aaaaahhhhh*,' shrieked Dr Hughes. He abruptly sagged and collapsed between us. I felt warm sticky blood pump over my legs and hands as I reached down to help him.

'Aaahh, shit, shit, aahh, shit,' he screamed. 'Oh God, it's taken half my fucking hand! Oh Christ!'

I knelt down beside him and whipped out my handkerchief. Working as well as I could in the dark, I bound up the bitten flesh. From what I could feel the demon's beak had scrunched off at least two or three fingers and half his knuckles. The pain was obviously unbearable, and Jack Hughes was twisting around and weeping with agony.

Singing Rock knelt down too. 'The creature has gone,' he said. 'It just faded and vanished. But I don't know what kind of spirit Misquamacus will summon up next. That thing was only a minor creature. There are far worse manitous than that.'

'Singing Rock,' I said, 'we've got to get Dr Hughes out of here.'

'But we can't leave Misquamacus now. I don't know what he'll do if we let him alone now.'

'Dr Hughes is in terrible pain. If he doesn't have that hand attended to, he's going to die. It would be better to lose Karen Tandy than Dr Hughes.'

'That's not the point,' said Singing Rock. 'If we let Misquamacus alone now, he'll destroy the whole place. Hundreds of people could die.'

'Oh God,' wept Dr Hughes. 'Oh God, my hand, oh God.'

'Singing Rock,' I snapped, 'I've got to get him out. Look, do you think you can hold Misquamacus off by yourself for a few minutes? Keep that fire away from us while I take him up the corridor, then I'll get him to a medic and come straight back.'

'All right,' said Singing Rock. 'But don't take your time about it. I need at least one other person on my side.'

I lifted Dr Hughes up to a standing position, and wrapped his injured arm over my shoulder. Then step by step, I helped him down the corridor towards the elevators. He groaned in pain at every move, and I could hear his blood dripping on to the floor, but I found a new surge of strength to carry us on.

There was no lightning, and no attempt to stop us. Perhaps this was what Misquamacus had wanted – to get

Singing Rock on his own. But as far as I was concerned there was no choice. Dr Hughes was too badly hurt to stay in the corridor, and that was all there was to it.

We finally made the elevator. Its small red light was still glowing through the darkness, and I pressed the button for UP. After an unbearable pause, the elevator arrived, the doors opened, and we flopped inside.

The light was so bright after the gloom of the corridor that it hurt my eyes. I sat Dr Hughes down on the floor, with his bitten hand across his lap, and crouched down beside him. We rose swiftly up to the eighteenth floor, and I helped him out.

There was quite a reception committee waiting for us in his office when I carried Jack Hughes inside. Wolf was there, with a party of male nurses and medics, all equipped with flash-lights. Two of them carried guns, and the rest were armed with crowbars and knives. A red-faced balding doctor, in a white coat and spectacles, was standing with them.

When I came in, they gathered round and gently lifted Dr Hughes off my shoulder, and laid him down on a couch in the corner of the office. Wolf called for a first-aid pack and antibiotics, and they gave Dr Hughes a quick shot of novocain to ease the agony.

The red-faced doctor came up to me and introduced himself.

'I'm Winsome. We were just about to go down and help you out. What the devil's going on down there? From what Wolf says, you have an insane patient or something.'

I wiped the thick sweat from my forehead. Up here, in the calm light of the early morning, everything that had happened in the fetid darkness of the tenth floor seemed totally unreal. But Singing Rock was still down there on his own, and I knew I had to get back with help for him.

'Pleased you could come, Dr Winsome. I can't explain it all now, but we do have a very dangerous patient down there, yes. But you mustn't come down with all these people and these guns.'

'Why not? If there's an emergency, we need to protect ourselves.'

'Believe me, Dr Winsome,' I said shakily. 'If you come down with guns, lots of innocent people are going to be hurt. All I need is that influenza virus.'

Dr Winsome sniffed. 'This is ridiculous. You have a wild patient down there, injuring our doctors, and you want an *influenza virus*?'

'That's all,' I said. 'Please, Dr Winsome. As soon as you can.'

He stared at me with bulging eyes. 'I don't seem to recall that you have any authority in this hospital, sir. It appears to me that the best solution is for me and these other gentlemen to go straight down there and catch this patient before he tries to take bites out of any more of us.'

'You don't *understand*!' I shouted wearily.

'You're right,' said Dr Winsome. 'I don't understand at all. Wolf, are you ready with those flashlights?'

'Right away, Dr Winsome,' said Wolf.

'Wolf,' I appealed. 'You saw what happened down there. Tell them.'

The male nurse shrugged. 'All I know is, Dr Hughes got hurt by that patient. We ought to get down there and sort it out once and for all.'

I didn't know what to say. I turned around to see if there was anyone else who could help me, but everybody in the office was ready for a vigilante raid on the tenth floor.

Then, from his couch, Dr Hughes spoke up.

'Dr Winsome,' he said hoarsely. 'Dr Winsome, you mustn't go. Believe me, you mustn't go. Just give him the virus. He knows what he's doing. Whatever you do, don't go down there.'

Dr Winsome walked over to Jack Hughes' couch. 'Are you *sure*, Dr Hughes? I mean, we're all armed and ready to go.'

'Dr Winsome, you mustn't. But please hurry. Give him the virus and let him do it in his own way.'

Dr Winsome scratched his bald and crimson head, then he turned and said to the rescue party: 'Dr Hughes is in charge of this patient. I have to bow to his better judgement. But we'll stand by just in case.'

He went over to the desk, and produced a thin glass

phial of liquid from a small wooden box. He held it out to me.

'This solution contains potent influenza virus. Handle it extremely carefully, or we'll have an epidemic on our hands.'

I took the phial gently in my fingers. 'Okay, Dr Winsome. I understand that. Believe me, you're doing the right thing.'

I was almost tempted to take a gun back with me, even though I knew it would be foolhardy and dangerous. But I did take a flashlight. I went swiftly back to the elevator, punched the button for ten, and sank into the darkness again.

When the doors opened, I peered cautiously out into the gloom.

'Singing Rock?' I shouted. 'It's Harry Erskine! I'm back!'

There was no reply. I kept my foot against the door of the elevator to prevent it from closing.

'Singing Rock?' I yelled again. 'Are you there, Singing Rock?'

I switched on my flashlight, and directed it down the corridor, but there was a corner in between me and the door to Karen Tandy's room, and I couldn't see any further than that. Perhaps Singing Rock couldn't hear me, way around here. I would have to go and investigate.

I knelt down and took off my shoes, and wedged them in the elevator door to prevent them from closing. The last thing I wanted was to be waiting for an elevator to arrive from the foyer while one of Misquamacus' grisly beasts came after me.

Then, keeping a pool of flashlight in front of me, I padded down the corridor towards Karen Tandy's room, and the battle of the medicine men. It was very silent down there – much too silent for comfort – and I didn't feel like calling out to Singing Rock again. I was almost afraid I might get a reply.

As I approached the door to Karen Tandy's room, the thick sickly odour of blood and death came crowding into my nostrils again. I directed a long jet of light all the way down the corridor into the distance, but there was no sign of Singing Rock. Perhaps he was in the room, having a face-to-face conflict with Misquamacus. Perhaps he wasn't there at all.

I stepped softly and gingerly over the last few yards, pointing the flashlight into the gore-spattered doorway of Karen Tandy's room. I could hear something stirring and moving in there, but I dreaded to think what it was. I came closer and closer, keeping to the far side of the corridor, and then I rushed forward and shone the light full and square into the room.

It was Singing Rock. He was on his hands and knees on the floor. At first I thought he was all right, but when I shone the light towards him, he turned slowly in my direction, and I saw what Misquamacus had done to his face.

Crawling with terror, I flickered the light around the whole room, but there was no trace of Misquamacus at all. He had escaped, and was somewhere in the pitch-black twisting corridors of the tenth floor. We would have to find him, and try to destroy him, armed with nothing but a flashlight and a small glass phial of infected fluid.

'Harry?' whispered Singing Rock. I walked across and knelt beside him. He looked as if someone had lashed him across the face with seven strands of barbed wire. His cheek was ripped up and his lips were split, and there was a great deal of blood. I took out my handkerchief and gingerly dabbed at it.

'Are you hurt bad?' I asked him. 'What happened? Where's Misquamacus?'

Singing Rock wiped blood from his mouth. 'I tried to stop him,' he said. 'I did everything I knew.'

'Did he hit you?'

'He didn't have to. He gave me a faceful of surgical instruments. He would have killed me if he could have done.'

I rummaged in the bedside cabinet and found Singing Rock some gauze and bandages. when the blood was wiped away, his face didn't look too bad. His own self-protective magic had managed to divert most of the scalpels and probes that Misquamacus had sent flying in his direction. Several of them were stuck in the wall, right up to the handles.

'Did you get the virus?' asked Singing Rock. 'Just let me stop this bleeding, and then we'll go after him.'

'It's here,' I said. 'It doesn't look much, but Dr Winsome says this little lot can do the job a thousand times over.'

Singing Rock held the phial up and squinted at it. 'Let's just pray it works. I don't think we have much time.'

I picked up the flashlight, and we stepped quietly over to the door of the room and listened. There was no sound at all, except for our own suppressed breathing. The corridors were deserted and dark, and there were more than a hundred rooms in which Misquamacus could have hidden himself.

'Did you see which way he went?' I asked Singing Rock.

'No,' said Singing Rock. 'Anyway, it's been five minutes. He could be anyplace by now.'

'It's very silent. Does that mean anything?'

'I don't know. I don't know what he plans to do next.'

I coughed. 'What would *you* do, if you were him? I mean – magically speaking?'

Singing Rock thought for a while, still patting his ravaged cheek with a bloodstained pad of gauze.

'I'm not sure,' he said. 'You have to look at it from Misquamacus' point of view. In his own mind, he left Manhattan in the 1600s only days ago. The white man, to him, is still a strange and hostile invader from nowhere. Misquamacus is very powerful, but he's obviously frightened. What's more, he's suffering from physical disabilities, which isn't going to help his morale much. I think he's going to call in all the reinforcements he can get.'

I flicked the flashlight up and down the corridor. 'Reinforcements? You mean more demons?'

'Certainly. We've only seen the beginning of this.'

'So what can we do?'

Singing Rock, in the reflected light of the torch, could only shake his head.

'There's only one thing on our side,' he said. 'If Misquamacus wants to bring demons out of the great beyond, he's going to have to prepare gateways to bring them through.'

'Gateways? What are you talking about?'

'Let me put it simply. Imagine there's a wall between the spirit world and the physical world. If Misquamacus wants to call any demons through, he has to remove some bricks from that wall, and prepare an entrance for the demons to come through. They need to be coaxed, too. Demons almost always demand a price for their services. Like the Lizard-of-the-Trees and his morsel of living flesh.'

'Morsel?' I said. 'Christ – some morsel.'

Singing Rock held my arm. 'Harry,' he said quietly, 'it's going to be more than morsels before we're through with this.'

I turned around and looked at him. For the first time, I realized what a trap we were in, and how there was only one way out.

'All right,' I said. I didn't want to say 'all right' at all, but it looked as if I didn't have any choice. 'Let's go find him.'

We stepped out into the corridor, looking left and right. The silence was oppressive, and I could hear the rush of air molecules bombarding my eardrums, and the pumping of my own heart. The sustained fear of encountering Misquamacus or one of his demons made us both sweat and shiver, and Singing Rock's teeth were chattering by the time we made it down the first corridor. At each door, we aimed the beam of the flashlight through the window, and checked to see if the medicine man was hiding inside.

'These gateways,' I whispered to Singing Rock as we turned the first corner, 'what are they like?'

Singing Rock shrugged. 'There are many different kinds. All it takes to bring a demon like the Lizard-of-the-Trees through is a circle on the floor and the proper promises and incantations. But the Lizard-of-the-Trees is not particularly powerful. He's just a minion in the hierarchy of Red Indian demons. If you want to summon a demon like the Lodge-Pole Guardian or the Water Snake, you have to prepare the kind of nexus that will make the physical world seem attractive to them.'

'Check that door over there,' I said, interrupting him. I flashed the beam his way, and he peered through the window into the hospital room. He shook his head.

'I just hope he's still on this floor,' said Singing Rock. 'If he gets out of here, we're in big trouble.'

'The stairway's guarded,' I pointed out.

Singing Rock pulled a tight smile. 'Against Misquamacus, nothing is guarded.'

We walked carefully forward down the corridor, stopping every few yards to investigate rooms, cupboards and odd corners. I was beginning to wonder if Misquamacus had ever existed, or if he was just a weird hallucination.

'Have you ever summoned a demon yourself?' I asked Singing Rock. 'I mean – can't we pull a few in on *our* side? If Misquamacus is going for reinforcements, why shouldn't we?'

Singing Rock smiled again. 'Harry, I don't think you know what you're saying. These demons are not jokes. They're not men dressed up. The greatest of them, the upper hierarchy of Red Indian demons, can take many forms. Some of them change their shape and their whole essence continuously. One minute they're like terrible bison, and the next they're like a pit full of snakes. They have no sense of human conscience and no sense of pity. Do you think that Lizard *pitied* Jack Hughes when it bit his hand off? If you want these demons on your side, you have to want something very pitiless done for you, and you have to disregard the possible consequences of something going wrong.'

'You mean they're all evil?' I asked him. I sent my flashlight beam up the corridor to probe a suspicious-looking shape. It turned out to be a hunched-up waste-paper sack.

'No,' said Singing Rock. 'They're not evil in the sense that we understand it. But you have to understand that the natural forces in this planet are not in sympathy with mankind. Mother Nature, whatever it said in your Sunday-school catechism, is not benign. We cut down trees, and the spirits and demons of the trees are dispossessed. We dig out mines and quarries, and disturb the demons of the rocks and soil. Why do you think there are so many stories of devils possessing people on isolated farms? Have you ever been around Pennsylvania, and seen the pentacles and amulets that farmers wear, to ward off the demons? Those farmers have disturbed the demons of the trees and fields, and they are paying for it.'

We turned another corner. Suddenly, I said: 'What's that?'

We peered into the darkness. We had to wait for two or three minutes before we saw anything. Then, there was a brief flicker of bluish light from one of the doorways.

Singing Rock said: 'That's it. Misquamacus is up there. I don't know what he's doing, but whatever it is, we're not going to like it.'

I took my phial of influenza virus out of my pocket. 'We've got this,' I reminded him. 'And whatever Misquamacus has in store for us, it can't be as bad as what we've got in store for him.'

Singing Rock sniffed. 'Don't get too confident, Harry. For all we know, Misquamacus is immune.'

I slapped his shoulder and tried to make a joke. 'That's right, bolster my confidence!' But all the time I felt as if every nerve in my body was tingling, and I would have done anything to relieve my watery, sliding bowels.

I killed the torch and we walked tentatively up the corridor towards the flickering light. It looked like someone was welding something, or the reflection of distant lightning. The only difference was, it had an unearthly quality about it, a strange coldness that reminded me of stars, when you stare up at the sky on a lonesome winter's night, and they're twinkling chill and distant and utterly remote.

We reached the door. It was closed, and the bluish light was shining through the small window in the top, and underneath. Singing Rock said: 'Are you going to take a look, or shall I?'

I shivered, like someone was stepping on my grave. 'I'll do it. You've done enough for the moment.'

I crossed the corridor and pressed myself to the wall alongside the door. The wall was oddly cold there, and when I got closer to the window in the door, I realized that there were spangles of frost on the glass. *Frost* – in an air-conditioned hospital? I pointed it out to Singing Rock, and he nodded.

Gingerly, I raised my face to the window, and looked into the room. What I saw there made my skin creep, and my scalp rise like a terrified porcupine.

# CHAPTER EIGHT

# OVER THE BLACKNESS

Misquamacus was sitting heavily in the centre of the room, supporting his deformed bulk on one arm. All the furniture in the room – which looked like a lecture theatre – had been tossed aside as if by a violent wind. The floor was cleared, and Misquamacus had drawn dozens of cabbalistic symbols and figures. The reincarnated magician had his left hand raised over the circle, and he was chanting something in hoarse, insistent whispers.

It wasn't the circle and the casting of spells that terrified me, though. It was the dim, half-transparent outline that appeared and disappeared in the centre of the circle – an outline of trickling blue light and shifting shapes. Shielding my eyes, I made out a curious toad-like shape that seemed to writhe and vanish, change and melt.

Singing Rock stepped softly across the corridor and joined me at the window. He took one look, and said: 'Gitche Manitou protect us, Gitche Manitou shield us from harm, Gitche Manitou ward off our enemies.'

'*What is it?*' I hissed. '*What's going on?*'

Singing Rock finished his incantation before he answered me. 'O Gitche Manitou afford us help, O Gitche Manitou save us from injury. Give us luck and good fortune all our moons.'

'Singing Rock – *what is it?*'

Singing Rock pointed to the hideous distorted shape of the toad-being. 'It's the Star Beast, which is about the nearest translation I can manage. I have never seen it before, only in drawings, and from what old wonder-workers have told me. I didn't think that even Misquamacus would dare summon that.'

'Why?' I whispered. 'What's so dangerous about it?'

'The Star Beast is not particularly dangerous in itself. It could destroy you without even thinking about it, but it isn't powerful or supreme. It's more like a servant to the higher beings. A go-between.'

'You mean that Misquamacus is using it like a messenger – to call on other demons?'

Singing Rock said: 'Something like that. I'll tell you later. Right now, I think we'd be well advised to get out of here.'

'The virus – what about the virus? Singing Rock – we have to take a chance and use it!'

Singing Rock moved away from the door. 'Forget the virus. It was a clever idea, but isn't going to work. Not now, anyway. Come on, let's go.'

I stayed where I was. I was terrified, but if there was any chance of destroying Misquamacus, I wanted to do it.

'Singing Rock – we can *threaten* him with it! Tell him that if he doesn't close that gateway, we'll kill him! For Christ's sake – it's worth a try!'

Singing Rock came back to the door and tried to pull me away. 'It's too late,' he whispered. 'Don't you realize what those demons are? They're a form of virus in themselves. The Star Beast will laugh at your influenza, and give you the worst death you can think of.'

'But Misquamacus—'

'Misquamacus may be threatened, Harry, but once he's summoned these demons, it's too late. It's more dangerous to kill him now than ever. If one of these beasts comes through, and Misquamacus dies, then there is absolutely no way of sending it back. Look at it, Harry. You want to risk *that* being loose in Manhattan?'

The Star Beast rippled and shimmered in its own ghastly fluorescence. Sometimes it seemed to be fat and glutinous, and at other times it seemed to be composed of nothing but sinuous clouds. It gave off an indescribable atmosphere of freezing terror, like a mad and vicious dog.

'It's no good, Singing Rock,' I told him. 'I have to try.'

Singing Rock said: 'Harry — I can't warn you enough. It's no use.'

But I had made up my mind. I put my hand on the ice-cold handle of the door, and prepared to open it.

'Give me a spell or something to cover me,' I said.

'Harry — a spell isn't a six-gun! Just *don't go,* that's all!'

For the space of two seconds, I wondered just what the hell I was doing. I am not the stuff from which heroes are usually made. But I had the means to destroy Misquamacus, and the opportunity, and somehow it semed easier and more logical to try and kill him than it did to let him go. If there was anything worse than the Star Beast, I didn't want to see it, and the only way to stop any more manifestations was to get rid of the medicine-man. I counted to three, and flung open the door.

I was not at all prepared for what it was like in there. It was so cold that it was like being in a dark refrigerator. And somehow, as I tried to rush forward, my legs could only move in a slow-motion, and whole minutes seemed to pass as I waded through the gluey air, my arm upraised with the glass phial of virus, and my eyes wide.

It was the *sound* that was the worst, though. It was like a terrible chill depressing wind, a note that was constantly falling and yet which never sank below a dull rushing monotone. There was no wind at all in the room, but that intangible hurricane screamed and roared and blotted out all sense of time and space.

Misquamacus turned towards me, slowly, like a man in a nightmare. He made no attempt to ward me off or to protect himself. The Star Beast, only yards away in the centre of the frosty gateway, shifted and pulsated like coils of toad-spawn, or twists of smoke.

'*Misquamacus!*' I shrieked. The words came out of my mouth like slow drips of melting wax, and seemed to freeze in mid-air. '*Misquamacus!*'

I stopped only two or three feet away from him. I had to hold one hand against my ear to try and blot out the deafening moan of the wind that wasn't there. But in my other hand, I gripped the infected phial of influenza, and held it up above me like a holy crucifix.

'Misquamacus – this is the invisible spirit which struck down your people! I have it here – in this bottle! Close the gateway – send back the Star Beast – or I will release it!'

Somewhere in the back of my brain I heard Singing Rock shouting: 'Harry – come back!' But the hurricane was too loud, and my adrenalin was pumping too fast, and I knew that if I didn't push Misquamacus to the brink, we might never rid ourselves of the wonder-worker, or his demons, or any of the fearful legacy from a magical past.

But I'm a clairvoyant, not a medicine man, and what happened next was something I just couldn't cope with. I felt something cold and wriggly in the palm of my hand. When I looked up at the phial, it had turned into a black squirming leech. I almost dropped it in disgust – but then a small warning in my mind said *it's an illusion, another of Misquamacus's tricks* – and I held it tight instead. As I gripped it, though, the wonder-worker outmanoeuvred me. The phial appeared to burst into flames, and my brain wasn't fast enough to override my nervous responses and reassure me that *this* was an illusion, too. I dropped the phial, and it sank slowly towards the floor – unnaturally slowly, like a stone sinking in transparent oil.

Terrified, I tried to turn away and run for the door. But the air was heavy and limpid, and every step was congealed into a massive effort. I saw Singing Rock in the doorway, his hands stretched out towards me, but he seemed to be miles and miles distant, a lifesaver on a shore I couldn't reach.

The writhing, colourless shape of the Star Beast had an irresistible attraction all of its own. I felt myself being physically drawn away from the door and back towards the centre of the magic gateway, even though I was using all my strength to try and escape. I saw the phial of influenza virus literally *change course in mid-fall*, and move through the air towards the Star Beast, tumbling and turning like a satellite falling through space.

Intense cold dropped itself over me, and in the dirge-like din of that windless wind, I saw my breath forming clouds of vapour, and stars of frost collecting on my coat. The phial of virus froze into crystals of glass and ice, which rendered it as harmless to Misquamacus as an empty gun.

I turned – I couldn't help turning – to look at the Star Beast behind me. Even though I was struggling across the room *away* from the gateway, my steps took me no further in the direction of the door. My feet were now only inches away from the chalked circle, and within the centre of the circle, the horrifying tangle of disturbed air that constituted the Star Beast was drawing me nearer. Misquamacus, his head lowered and his left arm raised, was intoning a long and deafening chant that appeared to exite the Star Beast even more. The monster was like the shadowy X-ray of a stomach, churning and twitching in digestive peristalsis.

I had been fighting to escape, but the cold was so bitter that it was difficult to think about anything else except how good it would be to get warm. My muscles ached with the frosty clutch of zero degrees and below, and the effort of running through the moaning gale and the oil-thick air was almost beyond me. I knew that I would probably have to surrender, and that whatever Misquamacus had in store for me, I would have to accept. I remember I dropped to my knees.

Singing Rock was screaming at me from the doorway. '*Harry!*' he yelled. '*Harry! Don't give up!*'

I tired to lift my head to look at him. My neck muscles seemed to be frozen, and the hoar-frost on my eyebrows and hair was so thick that I could hardly see anything at all. My hair was laden with frost, and there was a beard of icicles around my nose and mouth, where my breath had frozen. I felt nothing but a distant Arctic numbness, and all I could hear was the terrifying rush of that wind.

'*Harry!*' screamed Singing Rock. '*Harry – move, Harry! Move!*'

I raised my hand. I tried to struggle to my feet again. Somehow, I managed to pull myself a few inches away from the gateway, but the Star Beast was far too strong for me, and the magic charms of Misquamacus held me like a weakly-flapping fish in a net.

There was an electric typewriter, its keys thick with ice, lying on its side on the floor. It suddenly occurred to me that if I threw something like that at Misquamacus, or maybe at the Star Beast itself, it would give me a few seconds' diversion to pull myself free. That was how little I knew about the powers of occult beings – I was still treating them like cowboys and Indians. I reached out my frostbitten hands and lifted the typewriter up with tremendous effort. It had so much ice on it, it was nearly twice its normal weight.

I turned, I rolled over, and I hurled the typewriter towards the magic gateway and the dim outline of the Star Beast. Like everything else in this occult environment, it flew in a long slow-motion arc, turning over and over as it flew, and it seemed to take an age to reach the circle.

I didn't know what was going to happen. I just lay there, frozen stiff and bunched-up like a foetus, waiting for the moment when the tumbling typewriter would reach the Beast. I think I closed my eyes; I might even have slept for a moment. When you're freezing cold, all you can think of is sleep, and warmth, and giving in.

The typewriter reached the restless outline of the Star Beast, and then something extraordinary happened. In a glittering burst of metal and plastic, the typewriter exploded, and for a vivid second I *saw* something within that explosion. It vanished without a trace, but it was like an aggressive disembodied snarl. It had no shape and no form at all, but it left a fading mental image on the back of my eye, like a flash photograph taken in the dark.

The Star Beast *cringed*. Its serpentine coils and clouds seemed to roll back on themselves, like a ghostly sea-anemone. The mournful wind rose and fell in an odd, disturbed shriek, and I knew that if I was ever going to get away, it would have to be now. I heaved myself on to my feet, and scrambled for the door. I didn't look back, but I almost collided with Singing Rock, and the next thing I knew I was sitting blindly in the corridor outside, and the door was firmly shut. Singing Rock was making protective signs on the door to keep Misquamacus temporarily imprisoned.

'You're crazy!' said Singing Rock. 'You're absolutely crazy!'

I rubbed the melting frost from my hair. 'I'm still alive, though. And I did have a go at Misquamacus.'

Singing Rock shook his head. 'You didn't stand a chance. If I hadn't have bombarded Misquamacus with protective spells, you'd have been fried fish by now.'

I coughed, and looked up. 'I know that, Singing Rock, and thanks. But I still had to try it. Jesus, that Star Beast is so *cold*. I feel like I just walked twenty miles in a blizzard.'

Singing Rock stood up and looked through the door. 'Misquamacus doesn't seem to be moving. The Beast is gone now. I think it's time we got out of here ourselves.'

'What are we going to do?' I asked, as Singing Rock helped me on to my feet. 'More to the point – what do you think Misquamacus is going to do?'

Singing Rock shone the flashlight behind us for a brief instant, just to make sure that we weren't being followed. Then he said: 'I've got a pretty good idea of what Misquamacus is up to, and I think the best thing we can do is get ourselves out of here. If he's doing what I *think* he's doing, life is going to become distinctly unhealthy around here.'

'But we can't just leave him.'

'I don't know what else we can do. He's not making his magic as consistently and strongly as he should, but he's still too powerful to touch.'

We walked quickly down the corridors towards the elevator. It was dark and silent on the tenth floor, but our footsteps seemed muffled, like men running on soft grass. I was panting by the time we reached the last corner, and saw the welcome door of the elevator, still open and waiting for us. I dislodged my shoes from the door, and we pressed the button for 18. We lay back against the elevator walls in relief, and felt ourselves being carried upwards to safety.

There was quite a reception committee waiting for us when we stepped out into the bright light of the eighteenth floor. Dr Winsome had called in the police, and there were eight or nine armed officers standing around amongst the doctors and male nurses. The newspapers were there, too, and CBS television were just setting up their cameras. As we emerged from the elevator, there was a hubbub of questions and exclamations, and it was all I could do to push my way through.

Jack Hughes was sitting in the corner weith his hand heavily bandaged. He looked pale and sick, and there was a male nurse with him, but he had obviously refused to be sent off the battlefield.

'How is it?' he asked me. 'What's happening down there?'

Dr Winsome, redder than ever, pushed his way forward and said: 'I had to call the police, Mr Erskine. It seems to me there are people's lives at risk. I had to do it for the safety of all concerned. This is Lieutenant Marino, and I think he wants to ask you some questions.'

Behind Dr Winsome, I saw the now-familiar face of Lieutenant Marino, with his hard smile and his brush-cut hair. I waved, and he nodded back.

'Mr Erskine,' he said, pushing his way closer. There were five or six newspaper reporters clustered all around us, with their notebooks out, and the television people had just switched on their glaring lights. 'I just want to know a few details, Mr Erskine.'

'Can we talk somewhere private?' I asked. 'This is hardly the place.'

Lieutenant Marino shrugged. 'The press are going to get a-hold of it sooner or later. Just tell us what's going on. Dr Winsome here says you have a violent patient. Apparently he's already killed one man, injured this doctor here, and he's planning to kill some more.'

I nodded. 'That's true, in a way.'

'In a way? What's that supposed to mean?'

'He's not exactly a patient. And he didn't kill that man in the normal sense of murdering him. Look – it's impossible telling you now. Let's find ourselves a private office or something.'

Marino looked around at the press and the TV cameras and the policemen and medics, and said: 'Okay, if it's going to make it easier. Dr Winsome – is there an office we can use?'

The press groaned in disappointment, and started to argue about their right to know the facts, but Lieutenant Marino was firm. I called Singing Rock, and together we locked ourselves with Lieutenant Marino and his deputy, Detective Narro, in a ward sister's office. The press clustered around the door outside, and we spoke quickly and quietly so that they wouldn't hear.

'Lieutenant,' I said, 'we have a very difficult situation here, and I don't know how to explain it to you.'

Lieutenant Marino parked his feet on the desk and took out a Lark.

'Try me,' he said, lighting up.

'Well, it's like this. The man down there on the tenth floor is a homicidal maniac. He's a Red Indian, and he's seeking revenge on the whites.'

Lieutenant Marino coughed. 'Go on,' he said patiently.

'The only problem is, he's not a normal man. He has certain powers and abilities that ordinary people don't have.'

'Able to leap tall buildings at a single bound?' asked Lieutenant Marino. 'Faster than a speeding bullet?'

Singing Rock laughed, without amusement. 'You're nearer to the truth than you think, Lieutenant.'

'You mean you got Superman down there? Or Super Redskin?'

I sat up, trying my darndest to look sincere and believable.

'It sounds ludicrous, Lieutenant, but that's almost what we do have. The Red Indian down there is a medicine man, and he's using his magical powers in order to seek his revenge. Singing Rock here is a medicine man himself, of the Sioux, an he's been helping us cope. He's already saved several lives, and I think you ought to listen to what he has to say.'

Lieutenant Marino took his feet off the desk and turned around to look at Singing Rock. He puffed at his cigarette for a few moments, and then he said: 'Some detectives like wacky cases, you know. I mean, some detectives go out of their way to solve these real eccentric mysteries, and stuff like that. Do you know what I like? I like open-and-shut homicides. Victim, motive, weapon, conviction. So do you know what I get? Wacky cases, that's what I get.'

Singing Rock raised his lacerated cheek. 'Does that look wacky?' he asked Lieutenant Marino quietly. Lieutenant Marino said nothing, and shrugged.

Singing Rock said: 'I'm going to tell you this straight because we don't have very much time, and even if you don't believe me now, you will when things start to happen. My friend here is right. The man downstairs is a Red Indian medicine man. I won't stretch your imagination too far and tell you how he got here, or what he's doing on the tenth floor of a private hospital, but I can tell you that his powers are quite real, and highly dangerous.'

'Is he armed?' asked Detective Narro, a young, neatly-dressed cop in a blue suit and blue check shirt.'

'Not with guns,' said Singing Rock. 'He doesn't need to be. His magical powers are far more effective than guns. What's more, your guns will be quite useless against him, and potentially dangerous to yourselves. If I can't impress anything else on you, let me convince you of that. Please – no guns.'

Lieutenant Marino raised his eyebrows. 'What do you suggest we use as an alternative – bows and arrows?'

Singing Rock frowned. 'Your humour is a little out of line, Lieutenant. There's nothing funny about what's happening downstairs, and you're going to need all the help and all the information you can get.'

'Well,' said Lieutenant Marino, 'what *is* happening downstairs?'

'It's not easy to understand,' said Singing Rock. 'I'm not even sure of this myself. But here's the way I read it right now. Misquamacus, the medicine man, is preparing a magical gateway to summon Red Indian demons and spirits from the other side.'

'The other side of what?'

'The other side of physical existence. The spirit world. He's already managed to conjure up the Star Beast, which is the servant and messenger of the Great Hierarchy of Red Indian demons. Mr Erskine here – well, he saw the Star Beast with his own eyes, and nearly died.'

Lieutenant Marino said: 'Is that true, Mr Erskine?'

I nodded. 'It's true. I swear it. Look at the state of my hands.'

Lieutenant Marino peered at my blue and blotchy patches of frostbite and said nothing.

Singing Rock said: 'It isn't easy for any medicine man to conjure up beings from beyond. They're pitiless, dangerous and powerful. Most of the greater beings from Red Indian history are sealed off from us by ancient locks and spells that were imposed on them before the white man even placed one foot on our continent. The medicine men who locked them away in the spirit world were masters of their craft, and there isn't a single spiritual wonder-worker alive today who can match them. That's why these manitous are so perilous. If Misquamacus releases them, there is no one who can send them back. I'm not even sure that Misquamacus could send them back himself.'

Detective Narro was confused. He said: 'These beings – do you mean they're hiding in the building?'

Singing Rock shook his head. 'They are all around us. In the air we breathe. In the woods and rocks and trees. Everything has its manitou, its spirit. There are the natural manitous of the skies and the earth and the rains, and there are manitous in everything that is made or created by man. Every Indian lodge had its manitou; every Indian weapon had its manitou. Why do some bows shoot straight and others crooked? It depends on the faith of the man who holds the bow, and the sympathy he has for the manitou of his weapon. That is why your guns would be so dangerous to you. A gun has a manitou, according to whatever faith and craft has been invested in it, but your men do not believe that, and the manitous of their own weapons could quite easily be turned against them.'

Lieutenant Marino was still listening, but he was looking more and more miserable with every word that Singing Rock spoke. Detective Narro was trying to keep up with it, but it was plain that he believed that Misquamacus was a criminal maniac with a hidden gang. In Detective Narro's life, spirits and insubstantial shades from nether worlds just didn't exist. I wished to God that they didn't exist in mine.

Singing Rock said: 'From the gateway that Misquamacus is preparing, I think that he is calling on the most terrible of all spirits, the Great Old One.'

Lieutenant Marino said: 'The Great Old One? Who is the Great Old One?'

'He is the equivalent to your Satan, or Devil. Gitche Manitou is the great spirit of life and the Red Indian creation, but the great Old One is his constant enemy. There are many accounts of the Great Old One in ancient Indian writings, although none of them agree what he looked like, or how he could be summoned. Some say he looked like a huge toad, the size of several pigs, and others say he looked like a cloud with a face made of snakes.'

Lieutenant Marino sniffed. 'Kind of hard to send out an APB on that description.'

Singing Rock nodded. 'You wouldn't get the opportunity, Lieutenant. The Great Old One is the most ravenous and hideous of all demons. I have said that he's like your Satan; but Satan, by comparison, is a gentleman. The Great Old One is a being of infinite cruelty and malevolence.'

There was a long silence. Finally, Lieutenant Marino stood up, and adjusted his revolver in his belt. Detective Narro closed his notebook and buttoned up his coat.

'Thank you for your information and your assistance,' said Lieutenant Marino. 'Now I think we'll go catch ourselves a homicide.'

Singing Rock said, 'Lieutenant – you're not taking your gun?'

Marino simply smiled. 'Your stories about demons and all that stuff are very imaginative, Mr Singing Rock, but I have a homicide squad to run. The hospital has asked us to winkle out a mad patient who's already killed one nurse and injured a doctor, and it's my duty to go down there and get him out. Dead or alive, you understand, depending on how he wants it. What do you say his name was? Mickey something?'

'Misquamacus,' corrected Singing Rock quietly. 'Lieutenant, I'm warning you—'

'Warn me no warns,' said Lieutenant Marino. 'I've been

serving this force for longer than a coon's age, and I know what to do in situations like this one. There won't be no trouble, and there won't be no fuss. Just keep your heads down until it's all over.'

He opened the office door, and the press and the TV people came pushing in. Singing Rock and I stood amongst them, silent and depressed and frightened, while Marino gave a tough two-minute résumé of what he planned to do.

'We're going to seal off the the whole floor, then comb the corridors with marksmen and tear gas. We're going to do it real systematic, and we're going to issue regular warnings to this nut that if he doesn't come quiet he's in genuine trouble. I'm also sending three men down in the elevator to cut him off from that direction.'

The reporters scribbled down Marino's plan, and then bombarded him with more questions. Marino raised his hands for silence.

'I'm not saying anything else for now. Just watch how we flush him out, and then we'll chew the fat later. Is everyone ready, detective?'

'Ready, sir,' said Narro.

We watched despondently as a squad of eight armed patrolmen went to the staircase and disappeared through the door. Lieutenant Marino was standing by the elevator with his hand-held intercom checking for the moment when the search-and-destroy team would reach the tenth floor. Three men – two uniformed officers and Detective Narro – were waiting by the elevator, revolvers ready, all keyed up for the moment to go down there and shoot it out. After nine or ten minutes of restless waiting, there was a buzz from the men down below.

'How you doing down there?' called Lieutenant Marino through the intercom.

There was a crackle of static, then a voice said: *'It's dark. We can't get the lights to work. We may need some floods.'*

'Are you into the corridor yet?' asked Lieutenant Marino. 'Can you see anything?'

*'We're just through the door and we're ready to fan out and start looking. No sign of any trouble so far.'*

143

Lieutenant Marino gave the thumb's-up to Detective Narro and his two uniformed buddies, and they entered the elevator and pressed the button for 10. Singing Rock and I didn't look at each other as the doors slid shut and the floor indicator blinked 18 – 17 – 16 – 15 – 14 and down. It stopped at 10.

'How you guys doing?' asked Marino, into his intercom.

*'We're fine,'* came the voice of the search-and-destroy leader. *'So far there's nothing to report. We're going through every room, one after the other, and we're checking everything.'*

'Keep alert,' said Marino.

Detective Narro's voice, distorted by the intercom, said: *'It's very dark indeed. The flashlights don't seem to work properly. Does anyone know what's wrong with the lights?'*

Dr Winsome said: 'We've already checked. There's no fault that we can detect.'

Lieutenant Marino said: 'They say the lights have been checked and they can't help. Just be careful, and hold your flashlights away from your body. You don't want to make yourself an easy target.'

'Christ,' I whispered to Singing Rock, shaking my head. 'They still think they're fighting a mad gunman.'

Singing Rock was very pale. 'They'll find out,' he said grimly. 'I just hope it isn't too bad when they do.'

The voice of the search-and-destroy leader said: *'I'm having some trouble here. The floor-plan of these corridors doesn't seem to tally with the maps. We've been around in a circle twice, and it looks like we're just about to do it for the third time.'*

'Illusions,' said Singing Rock softly. A newspaper reporter with carroty hair looked up and said: 'What?'

'What's your position?' asked Lieutenant Marino. 'What room is nearest to you?'

*'Room Ten-Oh-Five sir.'*

Lieutenant Marino hurriedly consulted his floor-plan. Then he said: 'In that case, there should be a turning to your left, and then a right and you're into the next section.'

There was a brief silence, and then the voice said: *'Sir –*

'there's no turning. I mean, there's no opening. This is just a blank wall here. I can't see anything.'

'That's nonsense, Petersen. There's a turning right in front of you.'

'Sir, there's no turning. They must've changed the place around since these maps were drawn.'

Lieutenant Marino turned around to Dr Winsome, but Dr Winsome simply shook his head. Lieutenant Marino said: 'The hospital people say no. Are you sure that's ten-oh-five?'

'Affirmative, sir.'

'Well, keep on looking. There's probably been some kind of mistake. Maybe the suspect changed the room numbers around.'

'Sir?'

'Well, I don't know! Just keep looking.'

At that moment, there was a buzz from Detective Narro. His voice sounded oddly hoarse and strained.

'I think we have trouble here, sir.'

'What kind of trouble?' rapped Lieutenant Marino. 'Did you locate the suspect?'

'Sir – we're having some kind of a—'

'Narro? You're having some kind of a what?'

'Sir – we're—'

The intercom crackled for a moment, and then went dead. For a brief moment, I heard the mournful monotone of that wind that blew and didn't blow at all. Then there was silence.

Lieutenant Marino pressed his call-button. 'Narro? Detective Narro – can you hear me? Narro – what's going on down there?'

There was a buzz from the search team. Marino said: 'Yes?'

'Sir, we seem to have run into something here. It's extremely cold down here. I don't think I've ever been anywhere quite so cold.'

'Cold? What the hell are you talking about?'

'It's cold, sir. It's so cold. I think we're going to have to turn back. The flashlights won't work. It's very dark and it's very cold, sir, and I don't think we can carry on much longer.'

Lieutenant Marino jabbed the call-button and shouted: 'Stay down there! What the hell's wrong with you people? What the hell's going on down there?'

There was silence. For the first time, in that room full of newsmen and cameramen and medics, there was silence. Then, almost imperceptibly we felt the floor rise and fall like a passing wave, and every light in the room flickered briefly. There was a strange sensation like a cloud passing over the sun, and somewhere we heard the dull nagging sound of a mournful wind.

Lieutenant Marino went to the uniformed officer standing by the elevator doors. 'Get that elevator up here,' he said tightly. 'I'm going down to look for myself.'

The officer pressed the button and the elevator indicator rose up from 10 – 11 – 12 – 13 – 14. Lieutenant Marino tugged his police special out of his waistband, and stood by the elevator doors ready to step in when they opened.

The light on the indicator said 18. There was a hum, and the elevator doors slid back. There was a horrified gasp from everyone in the whole room.

The inside of the elevator looked like a butcher's frozen-meat store. The hacked and mangled remains of every policeman in the squad lay in a red, hoar-frosted heap. There were ribcages, arms, legs and torn-apart faces, all thickly rimmed with white crystals.

Singing Rock turned away, and I watched him turn away, and I felt as helpless and agonized as he did.

CHAPTER NINE

UNDER THE CLOUD

Half-an-hour later, we sat in Jack Hughes' office with Lieutenant Marino and Dr Winsome, smoking fast and drinking faster, and trying to think our way out of trouble. This time, Singing Rock and Jack Hughes and I were given something more than sceptical disinterest, and we told the police and the doctors everything we knew about Misquamacus and the strange dreams of Karen Tandy. I still didn't know if Lieutenant Marino was prepared to believe what we were telling him, but he had a slaughtered squad of police on his hands, and he wasn't in much of a position to argue.

The lights had started to flicker more regularly now, and that odd rippling motion of the floor was happening more and more often. Marino had sent out a call for reinforcements, but wherever they were coming from, they certainly seemed to be taking their own sweet time about it. Marino's intercom seemed to be growing fainter and less effective, and there was a persistent crackle on most of the telephones. A young uniformed officer had been sent out of the hospital to call for help on foot, but there was no sign of him, either.

'All right,' said Marino sourly. 'Supposing it's magic. Supposing all this garbage is true. What do we do about it? How do you arrest a manitou?'

Singing Rock coughed. He was looking tired and strained, and I didn't know how much longer he could keep going. The floor rose and fell underneath us, and the electric lights flickered an odd bluish colour. It was like travelling by ship on a heavy swell. The remote monotonous sound of the Star Beast's gale added to the impression of a desolate voyage into unknown seas.

'I don't know how we can stop Misquamacus now,' said Singing Rock. 'You can feel these vibrations. They're the preliminaries to the appearance of the Great Old One. According to the legends, the Great Old One is always preceded by storms and hideous minions. Dr Hughes can tell you all about those.'

Dr Hughes, without a word, passed over a black-and-white photograph that had been taken of his mutilated hand. He had disturbed the hospital photographic unit to have it printed up specially. Lieutenant Marino examined it without emotion and then passed it back.

'What do you think could have caused damage like that?'

asked Dr Hughes. 'Those are sharp, narrow teethmarks. A lion? A leopard? An alligator?'

Lieutenant Marino looked up.

Dr Hughes said: 'It could have been any of those. But how many lions and alligators are there in mid-town Manhattan?'

Lieutenant Marino shook his head. 'I don't know, doctor, and I don't really care. I'm very sorry about your hand. Believe me, I'm very sorry. But I'm a whole lot sorrier about eleven dead cops, and I want to do something about it. *Redfern!*'

A slight, bright-eyed young cop put his head through the door. 'Yes, sir?'

'Any sign of those reinforcements yet?'

'I've had a call from them, sir, on the r/t. They say they're having some trouble getting into the building.'

'They're *what?*'

'It was Lieutenant Geoghegan, sir, from the 17th. He said they would probably have to break down the doors. They can't get them open.'

Singing Rock and I exchanged glances. It looked as if Misquamacus had sealed the hospital off from the outside world. If there was one thing I didn't want to be, it was trapped in a hospital when the Great Old One made his appearance. Preferably, I wanted to be in New Jersey, or even Ohio. I shook my last cigarette out of its pack, and lit it with shaking hands. Again, the floor swelled, and the lights went so low that the elements fizzed.

'Call 'em again,' snapped Marino. 'Tell 'em we're desperate, and they better get their asses in here before the whole shooting-match goes up.'

'Yes, sir.'

Lieutenant Marino turned back to the meeting. He wasn't enjoying this job, and he wasn't making any pretence that he did. He picked up the bottle of bourbon, poured himself a heavy dose of it, and drank it with his eyes challenging everyone to say it was for medicinal purposes only. He wiped his mouth with the back of his hand and said: 'Right. I want to know every way there is of destroying the Great Old One. All the legends, all the bunkum, everything.'

Singing Rock shook his head. 'I can't tell you,' he said. 'Why not?'

'Because there's nothing to tell. There *is* no way of destroying the Great Old One. If there was, he would have been annihilated centuries ago, by those wonder-workers who were far more skilful than us. As it was, they only managed to close the gateway through which he came into the physical world.'

'And you say this guy Misquamacus is opening that gateway up again?'

Singing Rock shrugged. 'Can't you feel these ripples? Do you know what it is?'

'Earthquake?' suggested Marino.

Singing Rock said: 'No, Lieutenant. It's not an earthquake. It's the beginning of a huge build-up of astral energy. I imagine that, by now, the Star Beast has negotiated terms between Misquamacus and the Great Old One, and the nexus, the gateway, is being made ready. The gateway is made out of extraordinary energy, and only remains open for a short while. It takes an equivalent amount of energy to send the Great Old One back to where he came from. Even *more*, actually, because the Great Old One would be very reluctant to leave.'

'Sounds hopeful,' said Marino, sarcastically.

Singing Rock said: 'We can't give up hope yet. There has to be a way of containing the situation, even if we can't totally destroy Misquamacus.'

I crushed out my cigarette. A thought had occurred to me. I said: 'That typewriter I threw at the Star Beast – did you see that?'

'Sure,' said Singing Rock. 'It saved your life.'

'Well – when it exploded – when it actually touched the Star Beast's outline – I'm sure that I sensed something. It wasn't actually a face or anything as clear as that. It was more like a disembodied expression.'

Singing Rock nodded. He said: 'What you thought you saw was the spirit of the machine, the typewriter's own manitou. In its conflict with the Star Beast manitou, it became momentarily visible while it expended whatever energy it had. You can rest assured that the Star Beast thoroughly destroyed it.'

I frowned. 'The *typewriter* had a manitou?'

'Of course,' said Singing Rock. 'Everything does. A pen, a cup, a piece of paper. There is a greater or lesser spirit in everything.'

'I think we're getting away from the point,' said Lieutenant Marino testily. 'What we want to know is – how can we get rid of this Great Old One?'

'Wait,' I put in. 'This may be relevant. Why did the manitou of the typewriter come into conflict with the Star Beast? What did they have to fight about?'

Singing Rock pulled a face. 'I don't really know. The spirits are as much in conflict with each other as human beings. The spirits of the rocks are in conflict with the spirits of the winds and the trees. I guess it could have been something to do with ancient sorcery against technology.'

'What do you mean?' asked Jack Hughes, leaning forward.

'Simply that the Star Beast is a very ancient manitou, from times unknown,' explained Singing Rock. 'The manitou of the typewriter is part of the manitou of human electrical technology. They are bound to come into conflict. The spirit world mirrors the physical world to a remarkable degree.'

I thought for a while. Then I said: 'Supposing we had the technological manitous on *our* side? Wouldn't they help us? I mean – they'd be more inclined to support us than Misquamacus, wouldn't they?'

'I guess so,' said Singing Rock. 'But what are you getting at?'

'Look – if there's a manitou in every piece of machinery and human technological creation – we must be able to find a manitou that's able to assist us. The typewriter manitou was small and weak, but supposing we found one that was powerful and strong? Couldn't *that* defeat the Great Old One?'

Lieutenant Marino rubbed his eyes. 'This is too much for me,' he said tiredly. 'If I hadn't seen eleven of my own men killed and frozen in front of my eyes, I'd run you straight round to the nuthouse.'

Jack Hughes said: 'What you want is a machine with tremendous power. Something overwhelming.'

'A hydraulic power station? I suggested.

Singing Rock shook his head. 'Too risky. The Water spirits would obey the command of the Great Old One, and hold back your power.'

'How about an aeroplane? Or a ship?'

'Same problem,' said Singing Rock.

We pondered for a few more minutes. The floor began to sway even more violently, and pens and paper-clips skated off Jack Hughes' desk on to the floor. The lights dimmed, paused, and struggled on again. The floor heaved some more, and Dr Hughes' single Valentine card tipped over and fluttered under Lieutenant Marino's chair. I began to hear that monotonous wind noise even more distinctly, and there was a denseness, a closeness about the air that made me feel we were all going to suffocate. The heating system may not have worked too well in this office before, but now the place began to grow insufferably hot.

Officer Redfern came to the door. He said tensely: 'They're still trying to break in, sir. They came on the radio and they're still trying. Lieutenant Geoghegan said the building looks as if it's swaying or something. He says we got strange blue lights on the ninth or tenth floor. Shall I tell the rest of the men to evacuate, sir?'

'Evacuate?' snarled Marino. 'What for?'

'Well, sir, it's an earthquake, isn't it? In disaster drill, sir, they say that you're supposed to evacuate tall buildings.'

Lieutenant Marino slapped the palm of his hand on the desk. 'Earthquake?' he said bitterly. 'I wish it damned well was! Just round up two or three of the guys and see if you can help that idiot Geoghegan to get in. Take the stairs and watch out for the tenth floor.'

'Right, sir. Oh – and sir?'

'Yes, Redfern?'

'Detective Wisbech told me to say that he's run the m.o.

through Unitrak, and so far there's no precedent. No known murderer kills that way, sir. Not by freezing.'

Lieutenant Marino sighed. 'All right, Redfern.' He turned back to us and said: 'That's police efficiency for you. Eleven men get chopped up and chilled, and we have to run it through a computer to see if anyone ever went around doing things like that before. What the hell is wrong with memories these days?'

Redfern left, with a quick salute. The floor was stirring again, and he looked relieved to have been sent down to street level. What's more, the wind noise was moaning even louder, and how can you explain to people who hear gales blowing that there are no gales, and that the wind is the wind of occult malevolence?

'Just a minute,' said Jack Hughes, 'how did your detective get in touch with this computer?'

Lieutenant Marino said: 'By phone. The computer's available to all police forces in the state of New York. If there's anything you need to know about missing automobiles, missing persons, crime patterns, anything like that, it can tell you in just a few seconds.'

'Is it a big computer?'

'Sure. Unitrak is one of the largest on the Eastern seaboard.'

Jack Hughes turned to Singing Rock. 'I think we have found you a technological manitou,' he said. 'The Unitrak computer.'

Singing Rock nodded. 'That sounds more like it,' he said. 'Do you have the phone number, lieutenant?'

Lieutenant Marino looked bewildered. 'Now wait a minute,' he said. 'That computer is strictly for authorized police personnel only. You need a code to get through.'

'Have you got a code?' asked Singing Rock.

'Sure, but—'

'But me no buts,' said Singing Rock. 'If you want to catch the thing that killed your eleven men, then this is the only way to do it.'

'What are you talking about?' snapped Lieutenant Marino. Are you trying to tell me that you can conjure up a goddamned spirit out of a police department computer?'

'Why not?' said Singing Rock. 'I won't say it's going to be easy, but Unitrak's manitou is bound to be Christian and Godfearing and dedicated to the cause of law and order. Unitrak was made for that purpose. A machine's manitou cannot go contrary to the underlying intent with which it was fashioned. If I can summon it up, it will be perfect. History will repeat itself.'

'What do you mean – history will repeat itself?'

Singing Rock rubbed the back of his neck tiredly. 'This continent and its Red Indian spirits were defeated once by the white manitous of law and Christianity. I expect they can be defeated again.'

Lieutenant Marino was just reaching for his computer code card when the air seemed to go suddenly still. We looked around at each other uncertainly. The floor had stopped swaying, but now it was vibrating, very faintly, as if someone was drilling their way through concrete floors and floors beneath us. Way down below in the street, we heard sirens and fire-truck horns, and also the sorrowful moan of that magical wind.

Abruptly, the lights died. Lieutenant Marino shouted: 'Don't move! *Nobody move! If anyone moves, I'll shoot!*' We stayed frozen like statues, listening and waiting to see if we were being attacked. I felt drops of sweat sliding silently down the side of my face and into my collar. The rooms on the eighteenth floor were stifling and airless, and it was obvious that the air-conditioning had stopped, too.

I *heard* them first. Rushing and scurrying down the walls, like a phantom river. I saw Lieutenant Marino raise his police special in alarm, but he didn't fire. Chilled with fright, we peered through the luminous gloom of the offices, and saw them. They were like ghostly rats – torrents and torrents of scampering ghostly rats – and they were pouring down every wall. They emerged from nowhere, and disappeared into the floor as if it wasn't solid at all. There must have been millions of them – whispering and rustling and scuttling everywhere in a hideous tide of furry bodies.

'What is it?' said Lieutenant Marino hoarsely. 'What are they?'

'Exactly what they look like,' said Singing Rock. 'They are the parasites that accompany the Great Old One. In a spiritual sense, he is verminous, and these are the vermin. It looks as if Misquamacus is using the hospital building itself as a gateway to summon the Great Old One, and that's why they're pouring down the walls like that. I expect they're assembling on the tenth floor. After that – well, who knows?'

Lieutenant Marino didn't say a word. He simply handed his computer code card to Singing Rock, and pointed to the number on it. He seemed to be shocked and numbed, but then we all were. Even the newspaper reporters and the television crew were silent and apprehensive, and we stared at each other with the haunted eyes of men who are trapped in a sinking submarine.

Singing Rock went into a small side office and picked up the phone. I stayed with him while he dialled, and I could hear the ringing tone, and the click of the recorded answering machine. Squinting closely at Lieutenant Marino's card, Singing Rock read off a series of numbers, and waited to be put in touch with Unitrak.

'What are you going to do?' I asked him. 'How can you tell a computer that you need some help from its manitou?'

Singing Rock lit himself a small cigar, and puffed out smoke. 'I guess it's going to be a question of using the right language,' he said. 'And also persuading the programmers that I'm not totally crazy.'

There was another click, and a matter-of-fact WASPish voice said: 'Unitrak. Could you state your business please?'

Singing Rock coughed. 'I'm speaking for Lieutenant Marino of the New York Police Department. Lieutenant Marino would like to know if Unitrak has a spiritual existence.'

There was a silence. Then the voice said: 'What? Would you repeat that?'

'Lieutenant Marino would like Unitrak to state if it has a spiritual existence.'

There was another silence. Then the voice said: 'Look – what is this? Some kind of a joke?'

'Please – just ask the question.'

There was a sigh. 'Unitrak is not programmed to answer questions like that. Unitrak is a working computer – not one of your fancy university poem-writing gadgets. Now, if that's all?'

'Wait,' said Singing Rock urgently. 'Please ask Unitrak one important question. Ask it if it has any data on the Great Old One.'

'The Great What?'

'The Great Old One. He's a – kind of a criminal ring-leader.'

'What division? Fraud, homicide, arson – what?'

Singing Rock thought for a moment, then he said: 'Homicide.'

There was a silence. The voice said: 'You're spelling "Great" as in "Great Grief"?'

'That's correct.'

'Okay – hold on, then.'

Through the receiver, I could hear distant whirrs and clicks as Singing Rock's question was punched on to cards. Singing Rock smoked and fidgeted, and in the background we could hear the terrible sound of that spooky wind. The floor stirred again, and Singing Rock covered the mouthpiece with his hand and whispered: 'I don't think this is going to work. It won't be long now, and the Great Old One will be let through the gateway.'

I hissed: 'Is there anything else we can do? Any other way of stopping him?'

Singing Rock said: 'There must *be* another way. After all, the ancient wonder workers were able to seal the Great Old One in his own domain. But even if I knew what it was, I don't expect I'd be capable of doing it.'

As we waited for Unitrak, to come up with an answer, I began to feel an odd kind of nausea. At first I thought it was the swaying and rippling of the hospital floor, but then I realized it was a smell. A ripe, fetid, revolting smell that reminded me of a frozen rabbit I had once bought which turned out rotten. I sniffed, pulled a face, and looked at Singing Rock.

He's coming,' said Singing Rock, without apparent emotion. 'The Great Old One is coming.'

I heard shouting outside, and I left Singing Rock holding on to the telephone and went to see what was going on. There was a crowd of doctors and nurses around the CBS camera. I pushed my way through to Jack Hughes and asked him what had happened. He looked pale and ill, and his hand was obviously hurting him a great deal.

'It was one of the cameramen,' he said. 'He was holding on to his camera, and it seemed like he just collapsed. He was shaking like he'd had an electric shock, but it isn't that.'

I struggled forward towards the cameraman. He was young and sandy-haired, dressed in jeans and a red T-shirt. His eyes were closed and his face was contorted and white. His bottom lip kept shuddering and curling in a strange kind of snarl. One of the interns was rolling up his sleeves to inject him with a tranquillizer.

'What's wrong?' I said. 'Is he having a fit?'

The intern carefully inserted the hypodermic into the cameraman's arm and squeezed the plunger. After a few moments, the facial spasms and the shuddering seemed to die away, and apart from a few isolated twitches, the cameraman began to calm down.

'I don't know what it is,' said the intern, shaking his head. He was a callow young doctor with carefully-combed hair and a round, freshly-poured face. 'It looks to me like some kind of severe psychological shock. Probably a delayed reaction to everything that's been going on here.'

'Let's get him out of here and try to fix him up more comfortable,' called Dr Winsome. Three or four of the doctors went for a trolley, while the rest of us, frustrated and frightened, dispersed in awkward silence to wait for whatever manifestation was going to make its presence felt on us next. I heard Lieutenant Marino talking angrily on the telephone to his reinforcements, and it was clear that they were still having trouble gaining access to the building. Mingled with the moans of Misquamacus's wind, I could hear more sirens howling in the streets outside, and I could see spotlights flickering against the windows. In an hour or two, it would start to grow light, if we survived long enough to see it. The putrid stench of the Great Old One was thick in the air now, and two or three people were retching. The temperature kept fluctuating from stifling heat to uncomfortable cold, as if the whole building had a raging and uncontrollable fever.

I went back to Singing Rock. He was scribbling down a series of numbers on the corner of a magazine, and he looked intense and anxious. I waited for him to finish, then said: 'Do you think you can make it?'

Singing Rock examined the figures carefully. 'I'm not sure, but there's something here. The computer programmer said that the machine had no police records on anyone called the Great Old One, and he combed back for ten years through every known criminal alias. But Unitrak did respond with a message and a series of numbers.'

'What do they say?'

'Well – the programmer translated the message for me, and it says CALL PROCEDURE FOLLOWS PROMPTLY. Then we get the numbers.'

I wiped my forehead with stained handkerchief. 'Does that help? Does that mean anything?'

'I think so,' said Singing Rock. 'At least Unitrak answered. And if it answered – well, maybe it knows what we want.'

I pointed to the numbers. 'You mean these numbers tell you how to summon its manitou?'

'Possibly. We don't know until we try.'

I sat down wearily. 'Singing Rock, it all sounds too far-fetched for me. I know what I've done and I know what I've seen, but don't tell me that some publicly-funded computer is going to tell us how to raise its own spirit. Singing Rock, it just doesn't sound *sane*.'

Singing Rock nodded. 'I know, Harry, and I don't think I believe it any more than you do. All I can say is that the message from Unitrak is here, and that these numbers do tally with the appropriate ritual for summoning the manitous of man-made objects. In point of fact, it's the easiest of rituals. I was taught it by the medicine man Sarara, of the Paiute, when I was only twelve years old. I learned to raise the manitous of shoes and gloves and books and all kinds of things. I could make a book turn all its pages, without touching it at all.'

'But a book is a book, Singing Rock. This is a multi-million-dollar computer. It's powerful. It could even be dangerous.'

Singing Rock sniffed the stench of the Great Old One that was already crowding the room. 'Nothing could be more dangerous than what we are about to experience now,' he said. 'At least if we have to die, we will die a hero's death.'

'A hero's death doesn't interest me.'

Singing Rock laid his hand on mine. 'You didn't think of that when you faced the Star Beast alone.'

'No, but I'm thinking of it now. Twice in one night is too much for any man.'

Singing Rock said: 'What was all that noise outside? Was someone hurt?'

I reached for a cigarette from the pack on the desk. 'I don't think so. It was a cameraman from CBS. He was walking about filming and he just collapsed. I guess he must've been epileptic or something.'

Singing Rock frowned. 'He was *filming*?'

'That's right. I guess he was just taking shots of everybody in the whole place. He went over like someone had knocked him on the head. Don't ask me – I didn't see it.'

Singing Rock thought for a moment. Then he walked quickly out of the office, and over to the CBS reporters. They were standing in an uneasy circle, five or six of them, smoking and trying to figure out what to do next.

Singing Rock said: 'Your friend – is he all right?'

One of the reporters, a short stocky man in a plum-coloured shirt and heavy glasses, said: 'Sure. He's still with the doctors, but they say he's going to be okay. Say listen, do you know what the hell's going on here? Is this true, about evil spirits?'

Singing Rock ignored his questions. 'Is your friend prone to fits?' he asked intently.

The TV reporter shook his head slowly. 'Never saw him have one before. This is the first time, far as I know. He never said he was an epileptic or nothing like that.'

Singing Rock looked grave. 'Was anyone else looking through a camera at the same time?' he asked.

The TV reporter said: 'No sir. We only have this one camera here. Say – do you know what that terrible smell is?'

Singing Rock said: 'May I?' and lifted the portable television camera out of its case. It was dented where the falling cameraman had dropped it, but it was still working. One of the technicians, a dour man in blue denim, showed him how to heft it on to his shoulder, and how to look through the viewfinder.

The floor of the room began to tremble and pulsate, like someone shaking in fright, or a dog reaching a sexual climax. The lights dimmed again, and the sound of that gruesome wind grew steadily louder. There was a panicky babble from the twenty or thirty doctors and police and reporters crowded into the room, and Dr Winsome, ashen-faced and sweating, finally had to leave his clamouring internal phones off the hook. We didn't dare to think what was happening in other wards and offices, and we couldn't get to them now if we did. Lieutenant Marino was still hanging on to the phone waiting to hear from his reinforcements, but he had given up any semblance of optimism. He chain-smoked, and his face was set hard and grim.

As the floor spasm passed, Singing Rock pressed his eye to the black rubber socket of the television camera's viewfinder, switched it on, and slowly began to scan the room. He covered it in careful, systematic sweeps, exploring every corner and behind every door. The CBS crewmen watched uneasily as he circled the room, bent forward like a water diviner, his thin body tense.

'What the hell's that guy up to?' said one of the technicians suspiciously.

'Ssh,' said his colleague. 'Maybe he's trying to find out where the smell comes from.'

After a few minutes of careful searching, Singing Rock laid the camera down. He beckoned me across, and spoke to me in a low, hurried murmur, so that nobody else could hear.

'I think I know what happened,' he muttered. 'The demons which always accompany the Great Old One have passed through here. They are gone now – probably down to the tenth floor to gather around Misquamacus. But I believe the cameraman saw them.'

'He *saw* them? How?'

'You know the old story that Indians believe they should never be photographed, because cameras would steal their spirits from them. Well, in a manner of speaking that was correct. A camera lens, even though it can never steal a man's manitou, can *perceive* it. That is why there have been so many strange pictures in which ghosts – unseen when the picture was being taken – have mysteriously appeared when the picture is printed up.'

I coughed. 'You mean the cameraman saw these demons through the viewfinder? That's why he collapsed?'

'I think so,' said Singing Rock. We'd better go and talk to him, if he's still conscious. If he can tell us which demons he saw, we may be able to work out when the Great Old One is due to make his appearance.'

We called Jack Hughes over and explained what was going on. He said nothing, but nodded in agreement when Singing Rock suggested speaking to the cameraman. He had a brief word with Dr Winsome, and then he beckoned us through to the first-aid room.

It was silent in there. On a high hospital couch, the cameraman lay pallid and twitching while three doctors kept a close watch on his pulse-rate and other vital signs. They greeted Jack Hughes as we came in, and stood aside to let us gather round the cameraman's bed.

'Don't be too rough with him,' said one of the interns. 'He's had a bad shock, and he's not up to much.'

Singing Rock didn't answer. He leaned over the white-faced cameraman and whispered: 'Can you hear me? Can you hear what I'm saying?'

The cameraman simply shuddered. Singing Rock said again: 'Can you hear what I'm saying? Do you understand where you are?'

There was no response. The interns shrugged, and one of them said: 'He's deeply unconscious, I'm afraid. Whatever it was that happened to him, his mind has kind of retreated and it isn't coming back out for anyone. It's quite common in severe shock cases. Give him time.'

Under his breath, Singing Rock said: 'We don't have time.' He fished in his coat pocket for a necklace of strangely-painted beads, and he gently laid them on the cameraman's head, like a halo. One of the interns tried to protest, but Jack Hughes waved him away.

With his eyes closed, Singing Rock began an incantation. I couldn't hear the words at all, and those which I could hear were in Sioux. At least I presumed it was Sioux. I'm not a linguist myself, and for all I know it could have been French.

The spell didn't seem to work at first. The cameraman remained pale and still, his fingers occasionally twitching and his lips moving soundlessly. But then Singing Rock drew a magic figure in the air over his head, and without any warning at all, the cameraman's eyes blinked open. They looked glassy and ill-focused, but they were actually open.

'Now,' said Singing Rock gently. 'What did you see, my friend, through your camera?'

The cameraman shuddered, and there were bubbles of saliva at the corners of his mouth. He looked like a man dying from rabies, or in the terminal stages of syphilis. Something so terrible was imprinted on his mind that there was nothing he could do to exorcize it from his memory. He couldn't even die.

'It's – it's—" he stuttered.

'Come on, my friend,' said Singing Rock. 'I bid you to speak. It will not get thee. Gitche Manitou will protect thee.'

The cameraman closed his eyes. I thought for a moment that he had dropped back into unconsciousness. But after a few seconds, he began to speak – very quickly and almost unintelligibly – in a wordy rush.

*'It swam, it was swimming, it came swimming across the room and through the room at the same time and I caught a glimpse of just the edge of it like a sort of squid, like a squid, with waving arms, all waving, but it was big as well, I can't*

*say how big it was, I was so frightened there was something inside my head like my whole brain was stolen. Only a glimpse, though, just a glimpse.'*

Singing Rock listened for a while longer, but the cameraman said nothing more. He carefully removed the beads from the man's head, and said: 'Well, that seems to be it.'

'Is he okay? I asked. 'I mean, he's not—'

'No,' said Singing Rock. 'He's not dead. I don't think he'll ever be the same again, but he's not dead.'

'The squid,' I said. 'Do you know what that was?'

Singing Rock said: 'Yes. This man was privileged to see something that has been banished from the earth for centuries. He didn't see all of it, which is probably just as well. The Great Old One is among us again.'


CHAPTER TEN

## INTO THE LIGHT

I followed Singing Rock out of the first-aid room and into the corridor. His black eyes were glittering again with some of the zeal that I had slowly seen extinguished by our long and harrowing night. He said: 'This is it, Harry. Are you coming to help me?'

'This is *what*? What the hell's going to happen?'

Singing Rock licked his lips. His voice was breathless, and he looked as if he were feverishly ill. 'The Great Old One is here. To wrestle with the Great Old One himself – don't you understand what that means to a medicine man? It's like a Christian having the chance to fight with Satan in person.'

'Singing Rock—'

'We have to do it,' said Singing Rock. 'We have no time left at all. We have to go down there and do it.'

'*Go down there?* You mean – back to the tenth floor?'

Singing Rock appeared to grow in size, as if some magical

wind was inflating him. He was trembling with fear and anticipation, and the ultimate lust of risking his life against the greatest evil being of mythical America. When I said nothing more, he simply turned away and began to walk quickly towards the stairs, so fast I could hardly keep up with him.

I snatched his sleeve, and he turned around.

'Singing Rock,' I said. 'For Christ's sake – eleven armed men were killed down there. You saw what happened.'

'It's too late,' said Singing Rock. 'The Great Old One is here, and what happens now will be worse.'

'Singing Rock—'

He pulled himself away. He opened the door that led to the darkened stairway and said: 'Are you coming? Or are you staying behind?'

Echoing up the stairwell, I heard the loathsome moaning of that windless wind, and the hairs prickled on the back of my neck. The fetid stench of the Great Old One filled the air, and I could hear noises from down below that reminded me of Doré's engravings of hell. Demons and beasts and nameless things that walked by night. Things that drove men mad. Things that hopped and crawled and dragged themselves across the darkness of terrified imagination.

I swallowed hard. No matter how frightened I felt, I couldn't let Singing Rock go down there on his own. I said: 'I'm coming,' and pushed past him on to the concrete landing. If I didn't go now, I never would.

Once the door swung closed behind us, we were plunged into suffocating gloom. We held on to the handrail, and groped our way downwards stair by stair. Each shadow filled me with creeping fear, and every shuffle and echo made my heart tense up. I could have sworn I heard footsteps descending the stairs just out of sight below us, but there was no time to stop and listen.

'Singing Rock,' I whispered. 'What are we going to do?'

'I'm trying to think,' said Singing Rock quietly. 'But I can't judge the situation until I see it for myself. I just hope that I can invoke Unitrak's spirit at the right time, and in the right way. I just hope, too, that Unitrak isn't as hostile to us as it is to the Great Old One. There's always that risk.'

I coughed. 'Supposing we simply surrender? Wouldn't that save more lives? If we fight like this – God knows how many people are going to get hurt.'

Singing Rock shook his head. 'This is not a fight in the sense you think it is. This is an act of revenge by a Red Indian sorcerer in the name of all the pain and treachery and slaughter that his people suffered at the hands of the white man. You cannot surrender to someone who is seeking vengeance. Misquamacus will only be satisfied when we are all dead, and as for the Great Old One—'

'What about the Great Old One?'

Singing Rock shrugged. 'I don't know what bargain Misquamacus has made with him. But the Great Old One is known in Pueblo culture as the Great Devourer. The Paiute had another name – He-Who-Feeds-In-The-Pit. You can draw your own conclusions.'

As we descended through the darkness, the mournful whining and moaning of the wind that wasn't a wind became even louder and even more depressing. I began to develop a pounding migraine, and I could hardly see straight. I felt itchy and uncomfortable, and I had the feeling that my clothes were riddled with lice. If I'd had any choice, I would have given up then, and let the Great Old One, He-Who-Feeds-In-The-Pit, do his worst.

Singing Rock said: 'We're getting nearer. That's why you feel so bad. Here – take this bead necklace. It isn't much, but it should help to protect you against tricks and illusions.'

Almost deafened by the shrieking wind, we reached the tenth floor. Singing Rock produced the piece of paper on which he had written the numbers from Unitrak, and peered at them closely through the gloom. Then he gave me the thumb's-up, and gently pushed open the door that led into the corridors where Misquamacus lurked, and where now the Great Old One, the terrible malevolent manitou of centuries past, was hideously coming to life.

The stench was sickening. Even though the corridors were empty, there was a scuttling, rat-like noise everywhere – a noise that even the moaning of the wind could not drown. It was as if the whole place was alive with invisible rodents, swarming and clustering around the decaying smell of the the Great Old One. Singing Rock turned around to reassure himself that I was still behind him, and then led the way towards Karen Tandy's room – the room where Misquamacus had first made his obscene appearance.

The drone of the Star Beast's astral wind made me feel exhausted and irritable. As we came nearer to Karen Tandy's room, the noise grew louder and louder, until it sawed through all my senses with the coarse pain of a rusty blade. All around us, as we walked, there was the scuttling of ghostly rat-creatures, as if we had a loathsome escort of parasites wherever we went. Once, I felt as if one of them had jumped on my back, and I found myself tugging at my shirt in disgust and fear.

Singing Rock had begun his incantations. He was calling on the spirits of the Sioux nation to protect us from the devouring evil of the Great Old One; on the manitous of the air, the rocks and the soil; on the demons of sickness and plague to strike Misquamacus down. I could hardly hear what he was saying above the shrieking of that unearthly wind, but I could feel that our rat escort was treating us with a certain amount of impatient respect.

We turned a corner – and suddenly, the corridor was laced with brilliant flashes of light, which crackled and spat all around us. Singing Rock raised his hands, palm outwards, and the light poured against them and spent itself on the concrete floor. It was the lightning-that-sees – the first indication that Misquamacus knew we were here.

We reached the stretch of corridor in which Karen Tandy's room actually was. The lightning-that-sees seemed to have dispersed most of the phantom rat-creatures, but the groaning wind continued, and now it was a real wind, that blew against our faces like grit. Singing Rock beckoned me onwards, and we fought our way nearer and nearer to our inevitable confrontation with Misquamacus and the Great Old One. The shrieking and howling of the wind made it impossible for us to speak, and out of the door of Karen's room we saw sizzling flashes of astral light — the cold blue energy that had created the gateway for the greatest and most terrible of all legendary beings.

Then — against a tearing hurricane — we had reached the door itself. Singing Rock looked in first, and abruptly turned his head away in sheer terror, jerking his hand over his face like a man in the spasms of electrocution. I looked too, and I was stunned into such dread and fear that I felt as if I could never move from that doorway again.

The room was thick with evil-smelling smoke, pouring ceaselessly from two fires which Misquamacus had lit in metal bowls, and placed on either side of his astral gateway. On the floor was marked out the most sinister and bizarre circle of figures that I had ever seen, all elaborately drawn and coloured in what must have been the gore of Lieutenant Marino's police officers. There were strange goats and hideous creatures like enormous slugs, and naked women with loathsome beasts emerging from their wombs. Presiding over this circle, hunched and deformed, his dark body blurry through the smoke, was Misquamacus. But it was not Misquamacus himself that struck the greatest terror in us — it was what we could dimly perceive through the densest clouds of smoke — a boiling turmoil of sinister shadow that seemed to grow and grow through the gloom like a squid or some raw and massive confusion of snakes and beasts and monsters.

What was so terrifying was that I *recognized* the Great Old One — I recognized how close he had always been to me. He was the fright of strange shapes in a wallpaper and drapes; the terror of faces that appear in the grain of wooden wardrobes; the fear of a darkened stairs or curious and half-seen reflections in mirrors and windows. Here, in the writhing shape of the Great Old One, I discovered where all my long-buried fears and anxieties had come from. Every time you hear disembodied breathing in your bedroom at night; every time the clothes you have carelessly left on your chair seem to take the form of a sinister and monkish figure; every time you think you hear footsteps behind you as you climb the stairs — *it is the evil presence of the Great*

*Old One, straining malevolently at the locks and seals which keep him on the other side!*

Misquamacus raised his arms, and howled a chilling howl of triumph. His eyes seemed to be lighted from within, goat-like and satanic, and his body, on its stunted legs, was glistening with sweat. He had gloves of blood where he had torn bloodied bones out of Lieutenant Marino's men and used them to draw on the floor. Behind him, almost invisible in the smoke, the hideously frightening shape of the Great Old One twisted and squirmed.

'*It's now, Harry!*' screamed Singing Rock. '*Help me now – it's now! It's now!*'

He buried his face in his hands, and began to recite numbers and words, endless invocations to his own manitous and spirits, and the great spirit of white technology. I clung on to him, holding him tight, concentrating my terrified mind on *Unitrak – Unitrak – Unitrak*. The shrieking wind made it impossible for me to hear what Singing Rock was saying, but I pressed my mind into supporting him – into loving him – into keeping him safe while he tried to overwhelm Misquamacus and the murky presence of He-Who-Feeds-In-The-Pit.

There was a moment when I thought Singing Rock would make it. He was talking breathlessly fast, reciting and chanting and nodding, faster and faster as if building up to the great summoning of Unitrak's technological manitou. All this time, though, Misquamacus was chanting too, and sweeping his arm in our direction as if to encourage the Great Old One to consume us. I saw things move through the smoke that were frightening beyond belief – shapes more ghastly and dreadful than the worst nightmares I had ever had – and octopus-like coils of mist that began to unfold from the gloomy cloud of the Great Old One. I knew we only had seconds in which to survive. I was tensed up so tightly that my muscles were locked and I had bitten into my tongue.

Abruptly, Singing Rock slumped. He sagged, and then fell to his knees. I knelt down beside him, brushing my hurricane-blown hair from my eyes, and yelled at him to carry on.

He looked up at me, and there was nothing but fear on his face. *'I can't!'* he shouted. *'I can't summon Unitrak! I can't do it! It's a white man's manitou! It won't come! It won't obey me!'*

I couldn't believe it. I looked over my shoulder and saw Misquamacus pointing towards us with both hands, and the dark snakes of the Great Old One unrolling over his head, and I knew that this was the end of it. I snatched the crumpled fragment of paper from Singing Rock's hand, and held it up to the flickering astral light of the weird and horrifying gateway.

*'Unitrak save me!'* I shouted. *'Unitrak, save me!'* And I screamed out the numbers, again and again and again. 'UNITRAAAKKK! FOR GOD'S SAKE— UNIIITRAA-KKKK!!'

Singing Rock, still clutched in my arms, moaned in fear. Misquamacus, his face stretched in a wolfish grin, was actually *floating in the air* above me, his arms outstretched, and his deformed legs curled up underneath him. All around, the shifting and terrifying shapes of the Great Old One grew and grew.

I was silent with fright for a moment. Then – because it was all I could think of to do – I raised my own arms, just like Misquamacus had raised his, and cast my own idea of a spell.

*'Unitrak, send your manitou to destroy this wonder worker. Unitrak, protect me from harm. Unitrak, seal off the gateway to the great beyond, and dismiss this hideous spirit.'*

Misquamacus, floating eerily close, began to invoke the Great Old One in retaliation. His words sounded heavy and foggy, blurting through the howl of the hurricane like a vengeful beast.

*'Unitrak!'* I bellowed. 'Come to me Unitrak! Come!'

It was then that Misquamacus was almost upon me, and his devilish eyes glared luridly from his dark, sweat-glossed face. His mouth was drawn back in a snarl of pain and effort and revenge. He drew circles and invisible diagrams in the air around me, bringing down the evil tumult of the Great

Old One, arranging through his sorcery the most hideous of deaths that he could devise.

'Unitrak,' I whispered, unheard above the shriek of the gale. 'Oh, God, *Unitrak*.'

It was so violent and sudden when it happened that I couldn't understand it at first. I thought that Misquamacus had struck me down with the lightning-that-sees, or that the whole building had ripped apart around us. There was an ear-splitting sound that overwhelmed even the moan of the hurricane – an electrical crackling of millions upon millions of supercharged volts – a roar like a thousand short-circuits. The room was blotted out by a dazzling array of incandescent grid shapes – tier after tier of brilliant circuitry – crawling with white and blue sparks and shimmering with its own blinding symmetry.

Misquamacus fell from the air, charred and blacked and bloody. He dropped to the floor like a carcass of beef, his hands clutched up underneath him, his eyes tight shut.

The grids, pulsing and glowing, formed a fence between me and the murky shape of the Great Old One. I could see the demonic being shrink and twist – as if confused and frustrated. The voltage from the grid was so enormous that I could only look at it with my eyes half-shut, and I could hardly see through it to the twitching, shadowy form of the Great Old One.

There was no question in my mind what this blinding apparition was. It was the manitou, the spirit, the internal essence of the Unitrak computer. My spell – my white man's invocation – had brought the blinding retaliation of a white man's demon.

The Great Old One boiled and rolled in powerful coils of darkness. It let out a tortured groan that became an enraged bellow, louder and louder until I felt I was being swallowed by its deafening vibrant depths – a tunnel of screaming fury that made the walls shake and the floor tremble.

The glowing grid of Unitrak's manitou dimmed and flickered for a moment, but then it burned brighter still – a searing blast of technological power that blotted out all vision and all sound. I felt as if I had been plunged into a cauldron of molten steel, drowned in light and swamped in noise.

I heard one thing more. It was a sound that I can never forget. It was like someone or something shrieking in intense agony, on and on for longer than I could bear it. It was the sound of nerves being stripped bare, sensitivities being slit apart, spirits being carved naked. It was the Great Old One. It's grip on the material world was being scorched away by Unitrak's limitless and sophisticated power. It was being driven back by the holy fire of today's technology to the dim and dismal haunts of the ancient astral planes.

There was a rippling, bubbling, babbling noise, and the sides of the gateway that Misquamacus had marked on the floor began to draw in towards their centre, sucking in the shadowy shape of the Great Old One like a ventilation pipe sucking in smoke. There was one final extravagant burst of power that left me dazzled and temporarily blinded, and then the room was silent.

I lay there, unable to move, unable to see, for five or ten minutes. When I was able to struggle up to my feet, there were still green grid-shapes floating on my retina, and I had to shuffle around like an old man, bumping into walls and furniture.

At last my vision cleared. Not far away, Singing Rock lay on the floor amidst the debris of beds and broken furniture, his eyes flickering open as he gradually returned to consciousness. The body of Misquamacus lay where it had fallen, hunched and burnt. The walls of the room looked as if they had been seared by a flame, and the plastic venetian blinds were melted into long drooping strings.

It wasn't any of these things that transfixed me, however. It was the pale, slender figure who stood silently in the corner of the room – wan and white like a ghost of someone I once knew. I said nothing at all, but simply held out my hands to her – making her welcome back to an existence that she nearly lost for ever.

'Harry,' she whispered. 'I'm *alive*, Harry.'

And it was then that Lieutenant Marino, his gun drawn, came bursting through the door to find us.

I sat with Singing Rock at La Guardia, under the massive bronze bust of La Guardia himself, having a last cigarette, before he caught his flight. He looked as neat and tidy as ever, with his shiny suit and his hornrimmed glasses, and there was nothing to show what he had done, or what he had been through, except for a sticking-plaster across his cheek.

We heard jets taxi down the runways outside, and the murmur of voices, and the late afternoon sun glowed orange in a wintry sky.

'I feel a little sad, in some ways,' he said.

'Sad?' I asked him. 'What about?'

'About Misquamacus. If only we'd had a chance to explain to him what had happened. If only we could have communicated with him.'

I took a long drag at my cigarette. 'It's a little late for that now. And remember that he would have killed us, just as surely and quickly as we needed to kill him.'

Singing Rock nodded. 'Perhaps we shall meet him again, in better circumstances. Then maybe we could talk.'

I said: 'He's dead – isn't he? What do you mean – meet him again?'

Singing Rock took his eyeglasses off his nose and wiped them with a clean white handkerchief. 'The body died, but we can't be sure that the manitou was destroyed. Maybe it was released on to a higher plane, and is ready to join those who exist without any physical presence at all. Maybe it will come back to earth, and live again in someone else's body.'

I frowned. 'You're not saying that this could happen again?'

Singing Rock shrugged. 'Who knows? There are many mysteries in the universe that we know nothing about at all. What we see during our physical life on earth is simply a fragment. There are strange worlds within worlds, and stranger worlds within those worlds. It would pay us not to forget that.'

'And the Great Old One?'

Singing Rock collected his bag and stood up. 'The Great Old One,' he said, 'will always be among us. For as long as there are dark nights and inexplicable fears, the Great Old One will always be there.'

That was all he said. He took my hand, and squeezed it, and then went off to catch his flight.

It was nearly three weeks later before I was able to get out to New England. I drove all the way, and the fields and the houses were still blanketed with snow. The sky was the colour of gum, and an orange sun hid wanly behind the trees.

I arrived just before dusk, and pulled my Cougar up in front of the elegant white-painted colonial house and climbed out. The front door opened, and there was Jeremy Tandy, as dry and spry as ever, coming out to greet me and take my bags.

'We're so pleased you could make it, Mr Erskine,' he said, as warmly as he knew how. 'You must have had a cold trip.'

I wiped my feet on the doormat. 'It wasn't so bad. I enjoy adverse conditions.'

Inside, Mrs Tandy took my coat, and it was warm and firelit and cheerful. The long sitting-room was crowded with homely antiques – big colonial easy-chairs and sofas, brass lamps, and plenty of ornaments and pictures of rural scenes.

'Would you care for some hot chowder?' asked Mrs Tandy, and I could have kissed her.

I sat down in front of the fire. Jeremy Tandy poured me a large whisky while his wife busied herself in the kitchen.

'How's Karen?' I asked him. 'Is she still improving?'

Jeremy Tandy lowered his head. She can't walk yet, but she's putting on weight and she's much more cheerful. You can go up and see her later. She's been looking forward to this visit all week.'

I sipped my whisky. 'So have I,' I said, a little tiredly. 'I haven't been sleeping too well since this thing was over.'

Jeremy Tandy lowered his head. 'Well – no – none of us have.'

We made small-talk for a while, and then Mrs Tandy brought me the chowder. It was good and hot and thick, and I sat by the crackling fire and ate it gratefully.

Later, I went upstairs to see Karen. She was peaky and pale, but her father was right. She was putting on weight, and she was going to recover. I sat on the end of her country-quilted walnut bed, and we talked about her hobbies, and her future, and everything in the world except Misquamacus.

'Dr Hughes told me, privately, that you were very brave,' she said after a while. 'He says that what really happened was nothing like the newspaper stories at all. He said that nobody would have believed them if they'd told the truth.'

I took her hand. 'The truth isn't very important. I can't really believe the truth myself.'

She gave me a small, friendly smile. 'I just wanted to say thank you, anyway, because I do think I owe you my life.'

'Don't mention it. Maybe you can do the same for me one day.'

I stood up. 'I have to go downstairs now. Your mother told me not to tire you out. I think you're going to need all the rest you can get.'

'Okay,' she laughed. 'I'm getting a little bored with all this mollycoddling, but I guess I'll have to put up with it.'

'If you need anything, just tell me,' I said. 'Books, magazines, fruit. Just say the word.'

I opened the door to leave, and Karen said: 'De boot, mijnheer.'

I froze. I felt as if a pair of old hands had been laid on my back. I turned around and said: '*What* did you say?'

Karen was still smiling. She said: 'Be good, my dear. That's what I said. Be *good* my dear.'

I closed the door of her room. Outside, on the landing, it was silent and dark. The old colonial house creaked under the weight of the winter's snow.

'That's what I thought you said,' I whispered to myself, and went downstairs.

# THRILLERS

| 0426 | | Tandem | |
|---|---|---|---|
| | | Nick Carter | |
| | 173988 | THE DEFECTOR | 50p* |
| | 173392 | THE EXECUTIONERS | 50p* |
| | 157125 | HOUR OF THE WOLF | 40p* |
| | 173201 | THE HUMAN TIME BOMB | 50p* |
| | 157206 | THE KREMLIN FILE | 40p* |
| | 173120 | THE LIVING DEATH | 50p* |
| | 173716 | THE MIND KILLERS | 50p* |
| | 168704 | OUR AGENT IN ROME IS MISSING | 45p* |
| | 126262 | THE RED GUARD | 40p* |
| | 168895 | THE SPANISH CONNECTION | 45p* |
| | 125460 | SPY CASTLE | 40p* |
| | 174194 | TIME CLOCK OF DEATH | 50p* |
| | | Max Franklin | |
| | 147286 | NINETY NINE DEAD | 35p* |
| | | Michael T. Kaufman | |
| | 150422 | THE NICKEL RIDE | 35p* |
| | | Allan Morgan | |
| | 15181X | BLOOD — THE CAT CAY WARRANT | 35p* |
| | 147014 | BLOOD — THE SPANDAU WARRANT | 35p* |
| | | Michael Maguire | |
| | 172914 | SHOT SILK | 50p* |
| | | Jim Robinson | |
| | 146131 | TOGETHER BROTHERS | 35p* |
| | | Michael Stratford | |
| | 14533X | ADAM 12 — THE SNIPER | 35p* |

# CRIME

| 0352 | | Star | |
|---|---|---|---|
| | | "Joey" | |
| | 39837X | HIT 29 | 60p* |
| | 300019 | KILLER | 50p* |
| | | Donald Rumbelow | |
| | 398639 | THE COMPLETE JACK THE RIPPER (NF) (illus) | 60p |

# CRIME

| 0426 | | Tandem | |
|---|---|---|---|
| | | Elizabeth Lemarchand | |
| | 170725 | THE AFFACOMBE AFFAIR | 45p |
| | 170806 | ALIBI FOR A CORPSE | 45p |
| | 170644 | DEATH OF AN OLD GIRL | 45p |

*Not for sale in Canada